Daniel urged Satan forwards towards Trinity. No-Head raised the shotgun to his shoulder, took and fired. The snake was instantly cut in half, section writhing and thrashing, its head ing in mid-air. Trinity scrabbled to her feet, hold of Daniel's saddle and swung herself up Satan's rump. Satan trotted up the ridge.

lose call,' said No-Head.

niel could feel Trinity shaking where she held him with her arms around his waist.

that mocc'sin had bit me, I wouldn't be seein' Creek again,' she said pensively.

she spoke, Daniel remembered Matt's words as y parted from him north of Austin: *I don't wan t' find one of you was bit by a rattler, dro 'ed in a flood nor struck by lightning nor not'* .

' ll,' he replied, 'we did say we would watch out each other.'

ty smiled and replied, 'Well, I sure do owe you one

Coyote
★ ★ ★ ★
Moon

MARTIN BOOTH

Printed and bound in Great Britain by
Cox & Wyman Ltd, Reading, Berkshire

CORGI BOOKS

COYOTE MOON
A CORGI BOOK 0 552 55001 9

First publication in Great Britain

Corgi edition published 2005

1 3 5 7 9 10 8 6 4 2

Set in 12/18pt Sabon by
Falcon Oast Graphic Art Ltd.

Corgi Books are published by Random House Children's Books,
61–63 Uxbridge Road, London W5 5SA,
a division of The Random House Group Ltd,
in Australia by Random House Australia (Pty) Ltd,
20 Alfred Street, Milsons Point, Sydney, NSW 2061, Australia,
in New Zealand by Random House New Zealand Ltd,
18 Poland Road, Glenfield, Auckland 10, New Zealand,
and in South Africa by Random House (Pty) Ltd,
Endulini, 5A Jubilee Road, Parktown 2193, South Africa

THE RANDOM HOUSE GROUP Limited Reg. No. 954009
www.kidsatrandomhouse.co.uk

A CIP catalogue record for this book is available from the British Library.

In memory of B,
who showed me the real Wild West, and for
Jamie and Honor who are inheriting it.

Note: There is a glossary and pronunciation guide of unusual words at the back of the book.

Chapter 1

★

THE BOY
ON THE *BURRO*

By late afternoon, Daniel sensed the *burro* was gradually losing its strength beneath him. It had been dawn when they had last tasted water and, even then, it had been brackish and stagnant. Daniel had not drunk his fill, although the *burro* had, its head down and snuffling continuously for fifteen minutes. He had thought to fill the stone bottle hanging from the wooden sack cradle on the animal's back but decided against it. Better, he had considered, to die of thirst than the bloody flux.

The track he was following was well used. The hoofprints of cattle and the slots of white-tailed deer criss-crossed in the powdery dust. He might have long since given up hope, and prepared himself for death, were it not for the fact that, mingling with the various creatures' spoor, there were the hoofprints of a horse – a shod horse.

Every slat of the sack cradle pressed into his thighs and buttocks. No matter how he tried to adjust his position, they still dug into his flesh, giving him pins-and-needles in his feet and making his back ache. The monotonous swaying gait of the *burro* did not help.

All around, the air shimmered with heat and there was not the slightest breeze. When he looked across the still expanse of waist-high grass, at the copses of wind-sculpted mesquite trees and thickets of *huajillo*, they seemed to be almost liquid. Twice, they formed the backdrop of a mirage, a nebulous ship in full sail riding upon a silver lake.

His head throbbed. He kept nodding off, only to be jarred back to his senses by the *burro* slipping where the path ran along the crumbling rim of a dry creek, or stumbling over a rock or dead tree root. He knew he had to keep awake. If he fell asleep, he was sure it would be into his last slumber.

To concentrate his mind, Daniel tried to visualize his parents but realized he could not. He had forgotten what they looked like and could only conjure up the scar on his father's left arm and his mother's dark blue eyes, filled with merriment.

Suddenly, the *burro* broke into a trot that quickly became a clumsy, loping canter. Daniel pulled on the reins, yet to no avail. The animal was determined to be neither slowed nor turned. Daniel dropped the reins. There was no point in holding them. He hugged the *burro*'s neck, gripping the sides of the wooden cradle with his legs. The tall grass thrashed against his face. He closed his eyes and mouth, praying that his mount would not brush against a prickly pear cactus. A long spine could easily pierce his eyelid and eye. He pressed his face into the *burro*'s sweating neck. Then the lashing grass heads ceased and the *burro* swung round through a right angle. Daniel was thrown off its back and onto the ground.

He lay winded and afraid. If the *burro* had run off, he was done for. Yet, when he opened his eyes, the animal was standing guzzling hard at a wooden water trough. Moving into his field of vision came a dog's head. Its fur was gingery-brown and it was half-snarling as if not quite sure what to make of him.

Daniel moved his arms and legs to test he had not broken any bones. The dog ominously growled, deep in its throat. A long shadow fell across them both.

'Roja!' ordered a quiet voice. 'Go on! Git . . . !'

The dog moved away. Daniel looked up, squinting. Against the lowering sun was the silhouette of a man.

'You sure as hell ain't no mule-rider, boy,' the quiet voice went on. 'Y'all right down there?' A hand appeared, reaching towards him out of the dark outline. 'You wan' a hand up?'

Daniel accepted the offer. The hand was large and muscular, the skin rough from heavy work. It lifted him easily onto his feet.

'Thank you,' Daniel said, brushing the dust off

4

himself. It hung in dancing motes in the sunlight. 'I am in your debt, sir.'

'Much obliged, I'm sure,' responded the man.

'If you will excuse me,' Daniel replied.

He staggered swiftly to the water trough, nudged the *burro* aside with a punch to its ribs and thrust his head under the water. His battered bumper-brim hat came off his head and floated on the surface. Coming up for air, he snapped at the water as if biting off mouthfuls of it. He then cupped his hands to drink but, despite his thirst, did not. As if they had materialized from nowhere were a man, two women and a girl of about his own age. They stood in a line watching him. Beyond them was a corral containing a dozen horses, a small bunkhouse made of planks and what he took to be a sort of adobe ranch house with log walls inter-filled with mud under a roof of sod.

'Well, what have we here?' said the man. 'The Wild Boy of the Wild Horse Desert, if I'm not mistaken. What's your name, son?'

Daniel looked the man up and down. He was tall and wearing a grey long-sleeved shirt rolled up to his elbows, pants made of duck, dyed dark brown and held up by a pair of braces, and boots with a square toecap protected by a brass strip. On his head he wore a battered broad-brimmed hat whilst around his waist hung a belt bearing a holster containing what Daniel recognized to be a Navy Colt revolver.

Another nondescript brown-and-white mongrel, which had been lying in the shade of the ranch house, got leisurely to its feet, barked once and started to amble towards Daniel.

'El Sueño!' exclaimed the man. 'Go back t' sleep, y' lazy mutt.'

The dog promptly fell to the ground and lay on its side in the sun, one of its hind legs half-heartedly scratching in mid-air, a nerve trapped in its hindquarters.

'El Sueño's an ol' fool,' the man remarked affectionately. 'Don't you go mindin' him none. He barks but he's too idle t' bite. An' he ain't got many teeth left in that ol' head of his. More like t' gum you t' death as chew you. Now! What's your name?'

6

'Daniel.'

'Daniel what?'

'Just Daniel,' Daniel responded.

'And where're you from, Just Daniel?'

'Not here,' Daniel answered equivocally.

'Well, you're certainly a ret'cent young feller,' the man remarked, continuing, 'My name's Matt Gravitt, this here's my wife, Molly, and my sister, May-Anne Bramwell. As you can see from the shape of her belly, May-Anne's with child.' He lowered his voice. 'Her husband's gone to the Lord these last three months.' He put his hand on the girl's shoulder. 'This here's my daughter, Trinity. She's twelve. How old're you, Just Daniel?'

'About twelve,' Daniel replied evasively.

'This here man who got you to your feet is Mr No-Head Nolan,' Matt Gravitt went on. 'He's my head *honcho*. Over there' – he jutted his chin in the direction of the bunkhouse, on the wooden boarded veranda of which squatted three figures wearing ponchos and broad-brimmed sombreros – ''re my *vaqueros*, Beto, Miguel and Fredo. And that's it, th' full population of Dark Creek ranch, saving th' horses and th' hogs and two hundred or so head of cattle out in th' brush someplace.'

'When did you last eat and drink, Just Daniel?' Molly Gravitt enquired.

'I drank this morning and I ate' – Daniel paused to count off the nights he had spent travelling – 'four days ago.'

'Four days without a crumb!' Mrs Gravitt exclaimed. 'Well then, Just Daniel, you'd best come on in an' join us in our supper.'

Everyone, including the *vaqueros*, sat round a large table in the ranch house upon which Molly Gravitt had placed three loaves of bread, a dish of sweet potatoes roasted in the embers of the stove, a sliced melon and a large wooden bowl full of stew. They had all removed their hats except No-Head Nolan, the *vaqueros* leaving theirs on a rocking bench on the deep veranda. Molly Gravitt ladled a helping of stew onto a wooden plate and passed it to Daniel. Beto broke off a hunk of bread for him, smiling as he handed it across the table.

'So, Just Daniel,' Matt Gravitt asked, 'where

did your journey start?'

Indeed, where had it started? Daniel thought. In London? In Castries? In Galveston? And which journey? he considered.

'Corpus Christi,' he replied.

'That's eighty miles, give or take some,' Matt Gravitt answered. 'You done that on the *burro*?'

'No,' Daniel admitted bluntly. 'I walked about twenty miles and then I stole the *burro*.'

'That was a wrong thing to do,' Molly Gravitt declared sternly.

'They'll hang you if they catch you,' Matt Gravitt added and gave Fredo a brief nod. The *vaquero* rose from the table and went outside, the spurs on his boots chiming with each step.

'Yet they did not catch me,' Daniel replied matter-of-factly. 'There were over a hundred *burros* there. I heard it was a mule train starting south for Mexico. I deemed they could spare one.'

'It still ain't a Christian thing to do,' Molly Gravitt persevered.

Fredo returned and sat down, saying, 'He's no' branded, *señor*.'

'Looks like Lady Luck's been mindin' out for you, boy,' Matt Gravitt said. 'What were you doing in th' seaport of Corpus?'

Daniel made no reply and ate the stew. The tender and flaky meat had a rich, gamey taste to it.

'Where you headed?' Matt Gravitt continued, having received no response. He finished his food and pushed his plate away.

'I don't know,' Daniel said. 'I was just going. I had no specific destination in mind. There is no one place for me to go so I just went.'

He wiped his bowl clean with a piece of the bread. The others studied him for a long moment.

'Now, you mind my words, Just Daniel,' Matt Gravitt began with a stern tone. 'We don't know jack spit 'bout you 'cept your given name, you come from Corpus and you're a mule thief. I got to declare that don't fill me with much confidence where you're concerned. Last thing we want at Dark Creek is a soul that'd run off with one of our horses the minute our backs're turned.'

'I can't ride a horse,' Daniel confessed.

'Can't ride a *burro* neither,' No-Head Nolan observed somewhat caustically.

Daniel turned his attention to Molly Gravitt. 'Thank you, Mrs Gravitt,' he said politely. 'That was an excellent stew. May I ask what meat it contained?'

'Possum,' she answered bluntly.

As he was eating, Daniel became acutely aware of the girl intently watching him. She had straight auburn hair cut close to the collar. Her arms and face were tanned from a life obviously spent in the outdoors. Yet it was her eyes that Daniel noticed most. They were hazel-brown and as sharp and inquisitive as a squirrel's.

'You speak funny,' she said at last. 'You sure ain't a Tejano and you ain't an American, lest you come from th' East.'

'I'm English,' Daniel confessed.

'English!' Matt Gravitt exclaimed. 'Well, I'll be damned! You sure as hell is hot is a long, long way from Englan'.'

'Where're your mother and father?' May-Anne enquired. Until now, she had sat quietly at the end

11

of the table, her hands resting lovingly on the bulge of her pregnant belly, as if she was already caressing her baby.

Daniel paused and looked around the table. Over the months since he had left England, he had become an expert judge of character, realizing that not all men were necessarily as they seemed. Now, however, something he could not define told him he could trust these people, that they would do him no harm.

'I do not know the whereabouts of my parents,' he said. 'I was parted from them over a year ago.'

'A year!' Matt Gravitt retorted. 'What you been doing since then?'

Daniel chose not to reply.

'Well!' exclaimed Molly Gravitt. 'First thing tomorrow, Matt'll ride with you to Corpus and look for them.'

'We did not part in Corpus Christi,' Daniel said, 'but in London.'

There was a stunned silence, eventually broken by Trinity who said, 'You mean you've travelled . . . ?'

12

Again, Daniel made no reply.

As night fell, Daniel was shown to the bunkhouse by Beto. It consisted of a large, oblong room with an open stone fireplace at one end and a well-scrubbed table running down the middle. On either side was a row of two tiered wooden bunks made of rough-sawn planks. The windows were small with solid plank shutters on the inside. Daniel was allotted one of the bunks, his small blanket roll of clothes having been removed from the sack cradle on the *burro* by Miguel. Above the bunk was a shelf for his belongings. Hanging from a hook screwed into a beam above the table, an oil lamp, the wick turned well down, cast a meagre glow. More light came from the glowing fire in the grate than from the lantern.

After washing himself from a bucket alongside No-Head Nolan, Beto and Miguel, Daniel lay down under his blanket.

'*Buenas noches*,' Beto said. 'Sleep good, *señorito*. Tomorrow will be a hard day for you.'

Daniel quickly fell into a dreamless sleep which

was only once interrupted in the early hours by Fredo entering and Beto leaving the bunkhouse, carrying a rifle which he checked over by the faint glow of the lamp before going out.

At first light, Daniel was shaken awake by Matt.

'Time to rise,' he said. 'We ain't got no place for a lie-a-bed at Dark Creek. You only lied in today on account of my gen'rosity and your bein' fair tuckered out yesterday.'

Daniel looked around. The *vaqueros* and No-Head Nolan were nowhere to be seen. The bunkhouse was filled with the aroma of coffee. Beside the fire grate, a coffee pot bubbled. On the table was half a loaf of bread and a plate bearing a heap of scrambled egg, some crisped rashers of salted bacon, a ladle of beans and a large knob of butter.

'Break your fast,' Matt ordered.

Daniel swung his feet out of his bunk, poured himself a mug of bitter, black coffee and sat at the table. Matt positioned himself opposite Daniel, who broke the bread and, using his finger, smeared it with butter.

'So long as you stay here,' Matt declared, 'you earn your keep. We don't carry no dead wood hereabouts. But' – he grinned – 'you will – firewood. As soon as you've finished your repast, I'll show you round Dark Creek so's you know it. After that, you come back here, sweep out th' bunkhouse, attend to th' dishes, scrub down th' table, clean th' ashes out of th' grate – but make sure you leave some fire in there – get th' blaze goin' again, put oil in th' lamp, fill up th' bunkhouse water butt from th' well then come see me. You got it?'

'I've got it,' Daniel replied.

'An' you keep th' fire in by puttin' a big thick mesquite log on the flames once you got 'em dancin'. It'll smoulder all day . . .'

Daniel's meal over, Matt showed him round. Apart from the ranch and bunkhouse, the corral and the well by the trough, there were also two low barns and a pig sty with seven large, black pigs in it. Separate from this was a smaller sty occupied by a sow and a dozen piglets. A little way off from the buildings were two privvies, one for the Gravitts, the other for the *vaqueros*. Surrounded by a tall

15

cactus fence was a vegetable plot, each bed of plants served by a little irrigation channel. Further away was another much larger corral for cattle.

It was late morning by the time Daniel finished his chores. The bunkhouse done, Matt had then set him to chopping kindling for the house stove, manuring the vegetable plot with pig dung and watering it, filling up the water butt at the end of the ranch-house veranda, then working dubbin into a saddle and bridle. He had just finished this task when Molly appeared beating a saucepan with a ladle.

The midday meal was simple: bacon and beans, a mug of coffee and a chunk of freshly baked bread. Talk over the meal table centred on a discussion of the merits or otherwise of the ranch horses, eventually shifting attention to a gelding No-Head Nolan had acquired in Uvalde a fortnight before.

'How did you get that horse?' Matt asked.

'Aces over threes,' No-Head Nolan replied enigmatically.

'Gambling's wrong,' Molly interjected.

'If God'd intended us not t' play poker,' No-Head opined, 'He wouldn'a' given us th' pastes.'

'Does it not occur to you, Mr Nolan,' Molly replied tartly, 'that maybe – jus' maybe – it was Satan as gave 'em to you?'

'Well,' No-Head replied, 'that hadn't occurred t' me none, Mrs Gravitt, but it done give me a name for th' beast. Reckon I'll call 'im Satan.'

'Twenty-five bucks a fair price?' Matt asked No-Head, sliding a small stack of coins over the table, the newly minted coins shining in a bar of sunlight cutting across the wood.

'That's very gen'rous of you, Mr Gravitt.'

'What're you doin', Matthew Gravitt?' his wife exclaimed.

'If he's called Satan,' Trinity said, 'for one, I ain't ridin' 'im.'

'Nor me,' added her mother.

'None of you's ridin' 'im,' Matt cut in. 'Satan's Daniel's horse.'

'That's very kind of you,' said Daniel, 'but I already have the *burro*.'

'Now that's a sight I'd like to see!' No-Head remarked. 'A boy on a *burro* at th' round up.'

'That *burro*,' Matt declared, 'ain't going to carry

you far. He's old an' he's all in. Sure as snakes have scales, he was never goin' to make Mexico with that mule train. I reckon you done them mule drivers a favour. But don't you think I'm jus' bein' charitable. You can assume that Satan's by way of me payin' you.'

After the meal, Daniel was given the dishes to clean. He took them outside and began rinsing them in a bucket of water.

'That's not the way,' Trinity said, watching him. 'You wait.' She went into the ranch house to return with her cupped hands full of ash from the stove. Kneeling at Daniel's side, she went on, 'Look! You take a little water, mix it with a big pinch of ash and rub it round the dish. Then you rinse off in the bucket. Anything that's stubborn and won't shift, add a little bit of grit.' She did the cooking pot, adding some soil to the ash. 'Got it?'

Daniel nodded. Trinity, retreating to the veranda step, sat down and watched him.

'You sure have a load to learn,' she commented.

'Yes,' Daniel agreed.

'But you'll learn quick,' Trinity continued

confidently. 'You got to. There ain't no free ride on this here wagon.'

Daniel glanced up. Trinity was wearing an ankle-length skirt and what looked like one of her father's shirts. Around her waist was a belt from which hung a wood-handled Bowie knife in a leather scabbard. On her feet she wore heavy boots.

'I'll do my best,' he replied.

As he spoke, it occurred to him that this might just be the place to settle down. For the while, anyway.

Chapter 2

★

A HORSE
NAMED SATAN

Satan stood in the corral, a saddle on his back, the reins loosely draped across his neck. Daniel perched upon the top rail of the corral fence.

'Now this here's a quarter horse,' Matt began. 'He ain't so tall as a reg'lar horse. He's good for cattle work. See' – he stroked the horse's legs – 'he's got a mighty power in him, short 'n' heavy but he's no laggard. Turn on a dollar, too. Intelligent and sharp as a cactus prickle.'

Daniel climbed down from the fence and stroked

the horse's muzzle. It was like warm velvet. The horse snuffled his nostrils, turned his head and nuzzled Daniel's neck.

'You two'll get along just fine,' Matt declared. He patted the horse's neck. 'Well,' he added, 'what you waiting for? Get up on him.'

Daniel put his right foot in the stirrup and reached for the saddlehorn. The horse moved away from him.

'First mistake,' Matt remarked. 'Never mount a horse on the right side. He don't like it.'

Daniel, feeling a little sheepish, crossed behind the animal to its other flank.

'Mistake number two. Never walk behind a horse. He likes to see what you're doin'. Further, if he's an ornery cuss, he'll kick out and you'll get a dose of hoof. Might even kill you if he gets you in the head. Now, you take these reins here.' Matt handed them to him. 'An' get on up.'

Daniel slid his left foot into the stirrup, grabbed the saddlehorn and lifted himself up. The saddle leaned towards him under his weight. He swung his right leg over and sat in the saddle. It was spacious, almost comfortable. It was, he thought, a lot better than a sack cradle. Feeling down, he put his right foot in the stirrup, settling the bar firmly in the instep of his foot.

'Nope,' Matt remarked. 'Don't thrust your foot in so far. Ride with just th' ball of your foot in th' stirrup. That ways, if you fall off, your foot'll come out and you won't be dragged. That'll kill yer, sure as bitty birds lay bitty eggs.'

For the next hour, Matt taught Daniel how to ride a quarter horse, how to hold the reins loosely, start it walking, turn it by just leaning the rein on the side of its neck, bring it to a standstill. Finally, Matt opened the corral gate.

'A quarter horse,' he began, leaning on the top rail of the corral fence, 'is so named on account of it first bein' bred for quarter-mile sprintin' races popular 'mongst th' high-falutin' folk of th' state of Virginia. You ready to see what Satan here can do?'

Daniel felt apprehensive, but he nodded.

'Jam your heels hard in,' Matt ordered, 'for th' ride of your life.'

Taking a deep breath and making sure he had

both reins in his hand, Daniel jabbed his heels in. The next he knew, he was past the corral gate and galloping at full speed over the scrubby cleared land that surrounded the buildings. The wind hissed in his ears and made his eyes water. Beneath him, Satan was a smooth, thumping engine of muscle and power. The creature's hooves struck hard upon the parched earth. To keep his balance, Daniel waved his free hand about in the air.

Satan had almost reached the start of the brush when he began visibly to slow. By the time the horse arrived at the line of mesquite trees, he had reduced to a trot which soon deteriorated into a walk. He was snorting for breath, his nostrils flaring. Daniel gently turned him and walked him back to the corral. No-Head Nolan had joined Matt at the rail.

'So what d'yer reckon, No-Head?'

'I reckon, Mr Gravitt,' he replied, 'we'll shape 'im into a fair *vaquero*.'

Daniel dismounted, a taste of dust in his mouth. He spat to try to rid himself of it.

'You done good, Daniel. Real good,' Matt said. 'I'm proud of you. I really am. Now you cool ol'

23

Satan down, rub 'im off. He's done 'nough work for today. And don't you forget, he ain't some common horse. He's special. A quarter horse. Go a quarter-mile, then he gets bushed. An' he's yours.'

'While yer tend 'im,' No-Head advised, 'get t' know 'im. Talk to 'im. Maybe, tell 'im yer life story. An',' he added, 'when you talk to 'im, use his name plenty. Let 'im know he's Satan. Jus' like you would teach a dog its name, 'cept a horse's more intell'gent.'

With that, the two men walked away.

Daniel led Satan into the barn, removed the saddle and bridle, washed down his legs and started to comb him. The horse stood docile, occasionally lowering his head to drink from a bucket.

'Well, Satan,' Daniel said at last, feeling some-what self-conscious to be talking to a horse, 'it's you and me from here on. So' – he looked round: the only person in sight was No-Head and he was way over by the corral – 'I'd best tell you a bit about myself.' He lowered his voice. 'My name's Daniel Chance. I'm English and I lived in the county – that's like the state – of Kent. I had a sister but she died of the smallpox. She's in Paradise now with the angels. My father's name is James and my mother is Bathsheba. He was a carpenter and wheelwright. They owned an orchard but things got bad after my sister died. We got hungry, and could buy no food. Then my father was arrested for stealing. He stole a duck off a pond. It wasn't an eating duck. It was just there to be pretty. And there was a huge flock of them. My mother plucked and cooked it. That night, the bailiff called with the constable and three of the landowner's men. They found the feathers. My parents were beaten, tied together and thrown in prison. The bailiff's men didn't catch me though. I hid in the orchard grass. The landowner persuaded the magistrate to sentence them to transportation. That means being sent away, over the seas, never to come back.'

Daniel paused and walked round to Satan's other side. The horse looked back at him, as if he was actually understanding the story and would have asked questions had he been able.

'After my parents were transported,' Daniel went on, untangling Satan's mane, 'I found out they had

25

been sent to a penal colony, the Swan River Colony in the land of Australia. I determined to follow them and sneaked aboard a vessel I thought was bound there. It was not. It was sailing to the Leeward Islands in the Caribbean. I left her there and, after some months, took passage bound for Galveston, working as a cabin boy.' He paused and wiped a single tear from his cheek. 'I don't think I'll ever find my parents. Now I must make a life for myself and they do say Texas is a place of opportunity. So here I am.'

Over the next month, Daniel attended to his daily chores in the morning then, after the noonday meal, Matt taught him how to throw a *riata*, swinging the noose of stiff rope over a post, put a saddle and bridle on Satan, butcher a *javelina* Miguel shot out in the brush and dismantle, clean and re-assemble a 12-gauge shotgun. At other times, he practised riding his horse, taking him up to a full gallop, turning him sharply this way and that. When Daniel thought he had riding mastered, he began to try throwing the *riata* from the saddle, at first with

Satan stationary, later with him on the move. It was not long before the horse seemed to anticipate not only Daniel's instructions but even his thoughts.

When he mentioned this to No-Head, the man smiled and said, 'That's on account of his bein' a trained quarter horse. See, I won 'im off of a cowhand – a right buckaroo, he was – so it stands t' reason.'

The following afternoon, No-Head took Daniel aside after they had eaten their midday meal.

'You got one more thing to do with that Satan. Not every horse'll do it, but I reckon he's smart enough to learn. An' if you don't try you won't know.'

They went over to the corral, where the horses were standing in the dappled shade of live oak, and walked towards Satan. The horse was still saddled.

'Get up on 'im,' No-Head said.

Daniel did as he was told.

'Now listen good,' No-Head continued. 'A horse can be right intell'gent. Like a dog. He can obey commands. You watch my horse over there.'

No-Head clicked his tongue twice. His horse's ears went up. The other horses ignored him. He

27

clicked again and his horse ambled over to them. No-Head stroked his nose.

'You see that? Now, you walk ol' Satan here 'cross th' corral. Just before you pull 'im up you make a special noise, special just to you an' him. One you ain't goin' t' use else. Don't matter what it is. Then you give your command. Watch.' No-Head tapped his horse on its rump. It trotted off. He clicked twice again and said, 'Stop.' His horse came to an abrupt halt. No-Head clicked his tongue again and said, 'Walk on.' His horse started to walk.

'Now you train ol' Satan here. I bet he'll be as clever as a wily hound. Make th' noise, close to his ear, give th' command then do it. Go through th' procedure six times. If 'e ain't learned by then 'e never will.'

Daniel took Satan out of the corral and followed No-Head's instruction, wetting his lips and making a two-part whistle through his teeth in Satan's ear, saying, 'Stop!' and pulling the reins sharply in. In less than ten minutes, Satan was trained. Daniel repeated the exercise with the commands turn left, turn right and walk on.

'It works!' he told No-Head.

'Thought it might,' the cowboy replied. 'Knew 'e was a smart 'un when I first clamped m' eyes on 'im.'

For most of his time, Daniel kept himself more or less to himself. When the *vaqueros* sat outside the bunkhouse in the evening twilight, singing in Spanish to Fredo's accompaniment on his guitar, he did not join in. At meal times, he did not speak unless spoken to and was careful not to offer an opinion in any argument or discussion. At night, he slept facing the wall. Sometimes – when he was talking in a low voice to Satan – he sobbed quietly to himself. If he wanted to be alone, he bedded down in the straw in the barn, close to the horse, feeling the animal's warmth beside him as the night air chilled and smelling the sweet odour of Satan's breath.

Matt took the wagon and two horses and was gone for four days. Whilst he was away, Molly took control of the ranch, allocating the chores and seeing that they were completed. On his return, Matt unloaded sacks of supplies and other cargo then called everyone into the house. Upon the main table were two long, narrow wooden boxes. He prised one open with a crowbar and removed a brand-new rifle wrapped in greased paper. The scent of the lubricating oil filled the room. He held the weapon up for all to see, as a proud father might his new-born son.

'I got us two of these in San Antone,' he announced. 'Th' new Spencer rifle . . .'

'More rifles . . .' Molly remarked with a critical sigh.

'No, wife,' Matt replied. 'These replace those two old single-shot muskets.' He nodded at the weapons on the wall across the room. 'This here Spencer is a lever-action repeater. Magazine holds seven rounds. Fires a fifty-six over fifty centre fire—'

'How much?' Molly enquired, cutting into his hymn of praise.

'Adjustable rear ladder sight. Accurate as—'

'How much, Matt Gravitt?' his wife insisted.

'Forty dollars. The pair,' he added to soften the statement.

Molly stared at her husband. It was a moment before she responded.

'*How* much?' she exploded.

'That included two hundred rounds. And a cleaning kit,' Matt defended himself. 'An' two good-quality—'

'I don't care if they come with a side of prime salt beef and a *mariachi* band,' Molly exploded. 'We can't afford *four* dollars, never mind . . .'

Matt put his arm round his wife's waist and pulled her towards his side.

'Hear me out, darlin' bride.' He kissed her lightly on the cheek and turned to the others. 'An' y'all, too. I got some news in San Antone . . .' He let his wife go and sat down on the table, his face losing its smile. 'Big news. Seems they done hold a ref'rendum. Texas has broken from th' Union. Seceded, they call it. We's a republic again. More or less, anyways. The southern states've formed a confederation. A force under General Beauregard's been an' attacked Fort Sumter at Charleston.

Now, it's war between us and the Union. The South an' the North.'

No one spoke, each lost in his own thoughts. Daniel wondered what this might mean for him but came up with no answer. The *vaqueros* exchanged glances.

'We are with you, *Señor* Matt,' Beto said finally, breaking the silence.

Matt put his hand on Beto's shoulder and said quietly, 'I 'ppreciate that. I truly do.'

'Will th' fighting come this far south?' May-Anne wondered aloud.

'I reckon not,' Matt reasoned. 'Most'll take place up east – Virginia, the Carolinas, Kentucky, Tennessee – but it'll mean the troops in Texas will be withdrawn. In turn, that'll mean we'll be in for Indian trouble. And we can count on *banditos* from over the Rio Grande. Once the Blue Bellies're gone, there'll be nothin' to hold th' tribes or the Mexicans back.' He ruefully grinned at his wife. 'Forty bucks wasted?'

Molly took his hand. 'No,' she half-whispered, more than a hint of anxiety in her voice. 'Not this time.'

The following morning, Matt gave one of the Spencers to No-Head, taking the other for himself. No-Head went off to examine it with the *vaqueros* whilst Matt led Daniel and Trinity out into the brush half a mile from the ranch house. Sitting down on the slope of a low boulder, he leaned the rifle gently against the stone.

'I've a need t' talk t' you two,' he began, easing himself into a comfortable position against the stone. 'This situation ain't good. It ain't just a war, it's a civil war. That means it ain't Americans fighting Mexicans or *bandito*s or hot-under-the-collar Indian braves in their fightin' feathers and paint. It's Americans fighting Americans. The North wants t' outlaw slavery and the South don't. Simple as that. We're defendin' our way of life.'

'But we don't have no slaves,' Trinity observed.

'True 'nough,' her father replied, 'but up in th' cotton and t'bacco-growin' states they do, thousands of 'em. Without them there'd be no cotton or baccy.' He swatted a sand fly that had settled on his forearm. 'What I'm doin' now is teachin' you two youngsters how t' handle this 'ere weapon. Best you knows how before th' need arises for you to actually use it.'

His words set the hair prickling on Daniel's neck. Matt would not be wasting his time and ammunition on such tuition if he did not believe it necessary.

Holding the gun in one hand, Matt pulled a metal rod about a foot long out from the base of the stock.

'This here's th' magazine loading tube,' he began. 'You take it out by way of this handle in th' butt plate. That's th' bit that fits against your shoulder. Next, you put in seven slugs.' He produced seven cartridges from his pocket, slipping them one by one into the tube. 'These here slugs're .52 calibre,' he continued, handing one each to Daniel and Trinity for them to study.

The cartridge was about the size of Daniel's thumb and heavy, with a blunt lead bullet at one end and a brass detonator at the other. In between was a varnished cardboard tube.

Taking the cartridges back, Matt went on to show them how the back sight worked, how to line

34

the sights up on a target and how to hold the gun, fitting it snugly into their shoulder.

'If you don't put th' gun firm into you, snuggle it like a kitten with your cheek on th' stock, it'll make your bones real sore. It's got a kick to it. Not too bad but, when you fire standin' up, you lean forward some to take the recoil. Now, Daniel, you lie down on the dirt.'

Daniel did as he was told and Matt passed him the gun. It was heavy but he was able to hold it, his left hand under the point of balance in front of the breech. His next lesson was how to use the rear sight, setting the distance to the target.

When Daniel understood it, Matt took back the weapon and slid the loaded tube into the butt.

'Now to fire it,' he announced.

'Doesn't Trinity get a lesson?' Daniel enquired. He did not want to be seen to be monopolizing the Spencer.

'Don't you worry 'bout me,' Trinity exclaimed. 'I knocked one o' my milk teeth out with th' recoil of a musket.'

35

'Right!' Matt instructed. 'Push down on th' trigger guard-cum-lever.'

Daniel obeyed. The mechanism was firm but moved slickly.

'You've got a slug in th' breech now. With your finger off th' trigger, pull back th' hammer with your thumb.'

The hammer was stiffer than the lever but Daniel managed it on the third attempt.

'See that dead mesquite stump?' Matt asked, setting the distance on the sight. 'Aim at that and squeeze the trigger. Real gentle. Real slow.'

Daniel lined the leaf sight up on the foresight then on the stump. He squeezed the trigger with his index finger. At first nothing happened. Then there was a click, the hammer fell simultaneously, there was an immediate explosion and the butt of the gun slammed into his shoulder. A dense cloud of grey-black smoke suddenly enveloped him. It stung his eyes and choked him. His ears rang. As the smoke drifted away, he saw the top of the mesquite stump was shattered.

'Now that's what I call a dainty bit of shootin'.'

It was No-Head Nolan's voice.

'Well done,' Matt said. 'We'll make a real good shot out of you.'

Daniel stood up, holding the rifle in his left hand and rubbing his shoulder with the other.

'Gave a kick,' No-Head observed. 'The more you huddle it in, the less you'll feel it.'

The lesson ended with Daniel pushing the lever down and forward, ejecting the spent cartridge and automatically loading the next into the breech. Trinity took the gun, lay down on the ground, raised the rifle and fired. Daniel watched as a hole appeared in the mesquite stump.

Over the next week, Matt gave Daniel further instruction in how to get the best out of the Spencer. He learned how to judge distance to the target, how to fire rapidly, keeping the gun more or less on the target between shots. By the end of the second week, he could hit the mesquite stump three times out of four in just under twenty-five seconds, timed by Matt's silver pocket watch. Once he was familiar with the rifle, Matt taught Daniel how to load and shoot the Navy Colt revolver. It was nowhere near as accurate as the rifle but Daniel found he could handle it more easily. He also discovered he needed only one hand to hold and fire it. His muscles had been firming up since he had started working at the ranch.

Daniel was woken by the brief, shrill sound of a bird. Not recognizing it, he got out of his bunk, pulled on his trousers and, so as not to stir the others, left his boots off and tiptoed to the bunkhouse door, gently sliding the bolt. As he did so, the bird stopped calling.

Cautiously, he looked outside. All was quiet. Dawn had broken but the sun was not yet up. A flush of pink on the eastern horizon suggested that the sunrise was not going to be long in coming and that it was going to be another sweltering day.

The air was still and icy. He stepped onto the porch of the bunkhouse, the earth cool underfoot. In the corral, the horses were moving restlessly. A flight of bob-white quail broke from the brush on the far side of the barn, flying low with their wings whirring.

He could not put a finger on it, but something

told Daniel that all was not right. He scanned the brush carefully, watching for a movement. The horses' agitation suggested to him that there might be a bear on the prowl nearby. Seeing nothing, he went over to the corral. The horses were milling round, dust rising from their hooves. In the centre, only Satan stood stock-still, as if he were the ring-master controlling the others circling round him. The horse was steadfastly facing the brush beyond the high corral post-and-rail fence.

Daniel climbed onto the top bar of the fence and followed his horse's line of sight. He could see no reason for the horses to be alarmed.

Then, in the flat dawn shade of the live oak, something moved. Daniel strained his eyes but could see nothing. He jumped down off the fence and was in two minds about calling Matt when, first, he smelled a most peculiar and unpleasant odour reminiscent of putrid fish. Second, in the brush, he fleetingly caught sight of a man running fast at the crouch.

He turned to sprint for the ranch house but standing between him and the building was a man at least six and a half feet tall. He was almost entirely naked, his only clothing a sort of off-white soft leather pouch in which he hid his genitals. He was muscular, his biceps as bulging as had been those of a weight-lifter Daniel had once seen at a fair. His face was blotched by daubs of ochre with deep red circles round his eyes, his skin covered in black, red and white lines, his nose pierced with a thin sliver of white wood and his nipples with long grass stems culminating in seed heads. All over, his body shone with grease. His head was close shaven except for a patch of hair on top which was long and plaited, ending in a knot tied with a thong of leather. At his throat was a tight necklace of beads and small sea shells and in his fist he grasped a long knife with a bone handle.

Daniel's pulse thumped. He wanted to flee but terror had his feet glued firmly to the ground. He wanted to shout, yet no sound would come.

The man took a step towards him. His face was expressionless, his eyes like those of a snake, narrowed, staring and devoid of emotion.

Behind the man, the door of the ranch house

opened and Matt appeared, the Spencer repeater nestling in the crook of his arm. He might, Daniel thought bizarrely, have been stepping out to go bird-shooting. Behind him, the bunkhouse hinges squeaked.

'Stand still, Daniel,' Matt called softly. 'You're quite safe.'

The man before him shifted the knife in his hand, as if to get a better grip on it.

Daniel wanted to run but he sensed that, if he did, the next thing he would feel was the knife sinking to the hilt in his back.

For a moment the man did nothing then, with a feline agility, he spun to one side and sprinted towards the barn, disappearing behind it. Molly stepped out of the ranch house and, carrying several small bags closed with drawstrings, a folded blanket, some beef jerky and a little mirror, walked into the middle of the dusty area in front of the barn, putting the items down on the ground. Matt came over to Daniel.

'Who was that?' Daniel asked. His legs felt weak and his hands shook.

'Karankawa,' Matt replied. 'You don't see too many nowadays. Ain't many left. They live near th' coast, but you sometimes find 'em way inland. Now jus' you come inside th' house an' watch.'

'They smell,' Daniel observed as he followed in Matt's footsteps.

'That's on account of they cover their bodies with 'gator fat.'

For a moment, Daniel wondered if Matt was teasing him but the rancher added, 'It keeps th' skeeters from bitin' 'em.'

'What's in Mrs Gravitt's little bags?'

'Salt, flour, a few cakes of pemmican . . .'

They entered the ranch house. The fire was glowing in the pot-bellied stove, the air redolent with the aroma of frying bacon.

'Now you stan' here at th' winder,' Matt ordered Daniel. 'Keep back a little ways so's he don't see a face. Don't move none. Jus' watch.'

Daniel did as he was told. After about a quarter of an hour, the sun now well up, he saw a movement in the shadow of the barn. It was low and hesitant. Suddenly, the Karankawa broke from the shadows

42

running as fast as he might. Grabbing the blanket, bags, jerky and mirror in one movement, without hardly pausing, the man was gone again. Only the dust kicked up by his feet lingering in the air was left to show where he had been.

''portant lesson,' Matt said. 'Don't forget it. If th' natives come in any way other than brandishin' their weapons, give 'em a gift. Nothing big. An' nothin' they can use 'gainst you, like a knife. That way, a conflict's avoided an' you might even make a friend or two, 'specially th' Karankawas. Those poor devils're near t' starvin'.'

'What's pemmican?' Daniel enquired.

'You sure has a lot o' learning to do,' Trinity remarked. 'You get dry strips of meat an' you grind 'em to a powder. Then you add powdered herbs an' dry berries an' the like. Then you render some fat right down an' add th' powder of meat an' such. Then you pour it into moulds an' it gets hard. An' you eat it. It's real good for you.'

Daniel sat on the log outside the bunkhouse. Beside him, Fredo strummed his guitar and sang a mournful melody as the dusk deepened. Out in the brush somewhere, a steer was belling.

'What are you singing?' he asked Fredo as the *vaquero* stopped to shift his hold on the instrument.

'Is a sad song, *señorito*,' he answered, 'about love and sorrow.' He put the guitar down, leaning it against the log. 'You know of much sorrow, I think, *señorito*. Is true?'

'Is true,' Daniel repeated.

'You know,' Fredo responded, 'some time it is good to talk away the sorrow. See.' He picked up two pebbles from the dusty earth. 'The stones are sorrow. I give you one.' He handed a pebble to Daniel. 'Now, I have only half sorrow. My sorrow small.'

'But then,' Daniel said, 'I have half your sorrow. The sorrow hasn't gone away. It's merely shared.'

Fredo sat up, flexed his biceps, puffed his chest out and declared, 'I am strong. I can carry sorrow you give me.'

Daniel did not reply. He looked ahead, beyond the ranch house to where the horizon was darkening with the night. Although the last of the sun was yet to leave the sky, the brightest stars were already glimmering overhead.

The door of the ranch house slammed open.

'Daniel!' It was Matt's voice. 'Get over here double-quick!'

Jumping to his feet, Daniel ran to the ranch house, grateful to escape a conversation he was sure was about to delve into his past, a past he would rather forget.

The main room of the ranch house was empty.

'In here!' came Matt's voice from a doorway at the back.

Daniel went through the door to find himself in a room containing a cast-iron double bed and a low, three-drawer wooden cupboard with a carved front. Two chairs had been brought in from the meal table. The walls were covered from floor to ceiling with nailed-up lengths of hessian sacking, the window shuttered and the air close with the smell of kerosene coming from a hurricane lantern standing on the cupboard.

May-Anne was sitting in the bed propped up by pillows, her legs arched, wide apart and covered for modesty's sake by a sheet. Trinity sat at her side on a chair, holding her hand. Molly stood on the other side of the bed.

'Her time's come,' Matt stated frankly. 'An' it's all han's to. Your job's t' keep hot water comin'. Not so hot as it burns. Just so hot as your skin can take it. When you've enough t' fill th' ewer, bring it t' th' door and holler out. Trinity'll come an' get it.'

For two hours, Daniel collected water from the butt, heated it and filled the ewer. From the other room came intermittent moaning interspersed by the occasional short scream, cut off as if by a gag. Murmured voices, too low for Daniel to comprehend, gave May-Anne support and comfort. Outside on the veranda, the *vaqueros* stood quietly. Daniel could hear Fredo muttering prayers in Spanish, and the muted clack of the polished beads as Beto fingered his rosary.

Just before eleven o'clock, May-Anne let out a prolonged scream which ran up Daniel's spine. It was high-pitched, unearthly, like the screech of a dying man. He felt himself start to tremble; then, a short while after it ceased, there was the muted caterwaul of a new-born infant. Matt came out of the room, his hands and forearms bloody.

'Bring that water outside, Daniel,' he ordered abruptly, 'an' sluice me down.'

Daniel stood on the dusty earth and poured the hot water over Matt's arms. Matt scrubbed at his skin with a bar of coarse soap then stripped his shirt off. It was spattered with blood. Walking to the trough, Matt dunked the garment in the cold water.

'Leave it there overnight. Ain't no one here t' steal it.'

Molly appeared in the ranch-house door, outlined against the lamp behind her. She stepped out from beneath the porch roof and held up something swaddled in a blanket.

'Lord God!' she said in a loud voice. 'I give unto thee Thadeus Bramwell an' ask that you mind for him an' see he come t' no harm.'

Above, the sky was a panoply of stars. Way off in the brush, a horned owl hooted melodiously.

Beto and Fredo crossed themselves. Molly lowered the infant and everyone stepped close to see the new-born boy. By the light of the lantern, he was bright pink with a faint down of dark hair on his crown, his skin crumpled and still damp. His eyes were screwed tight and one tiny hand gripped the blanket.

'Jus' think, Daniel,' Matt said softly. 'But fifteen minutes into this world . . .'

'. . . an',' No-Head added, 'I trus' a long, long time from th' next.'

Chapter 3

★

TO BE A COWBOY

Somehow, Daniel had expected the cattle to be bunched together. That was, he recalled, how cows appeared in the fields of his native Kent, moving slowly and in a docile manner across the green, dew-wet grass. Matt's cattle were spread out over two square miles of desiccated scrubby brush and it took him, No-Head and the *vaqueros* the better part of a morning to round them up. As they brought the beasts together, it was Daniel and Trinity's job to keep them that way by riding round and round them. Every so often, one of the cattle would break out and make a run for a thick patch of brush. Trinity, spurring her quarter horse hard, would head it off, turning it back into the herd.

The steers, as Trinity called them, were different from English cattle. They were lean and muscular, had massive horns up to five feet across and could run as fast as a pony. Of different coloured hides – brown, white, black, mottled – some of them were wily, too. If they saw one of the *vaqueros* approaching on his horse, they slunk into the bushes, not just to hide but because they knew, in the cover, they could not be roped.

'What exactly are we are going to do with them when they're all together?' Daniel asked.

'Don't be so 'quisitive,' Trinity replied teasingly. 'You'll see soon 'nough.'

Finally, about a hundred head of cattle were rounded up, many of them running with calves at heel. They were then driven into a wide U-shaped area enclosed on three sides by a stout, makeshift fence within and before which was a broad dusty area. To one side of the opening, Beto and Fredo set up a metal grill between four stones, piling dry brushwood beneath it. With a fire lit and blazing, they thrust a five-foot-long iron rod into the embers.

'Now th' real bisniz of th' day begins,' No-Head declared. 'By nightfall, young Daniel, you ain't gonna be no En'lish lad no more. You'll be a one-hun'red-per-cent, dyed-in-th'-wool Texas cowhand.'

Daniel smiled uncertainly at No-Head.

Matt rode over, reining his horse up beside Satan.

'This is where you put to practice all you've jus' been playin' at till now,' he said to Daniel and he pointed to the herd of cattle through which Miguel was riding slowly, his horse edging a cow and calf towards the entrance to the corral. After a minute or so, the cow and her offspring sauntered through the opening and out into the dusty area.

'Your job now, Daniel, is to cut that calf.'

'Cut it?' Daniel repeated.

'Separate it from its mama' – Matt nodded at the *riata* hanging from Daniel's saddle by a twisted thong of leather – 'then rope it.'

'But—' Daniel began.

'You ride ol' Satan towards them two an' . . .'
Matt interrupted him. 'Well, jus' you do it.'

Daniel turned Satan's head and the horse, without bidding, started to trot towards the cow and
her calf, gradually accelerating to a slow canter.
Suddenly, the cow kicked and started to tear away as
fast as it could go. The calf kept up, close to its
mother's side. Satan broke into a full gallop. As the
cow veered to one side, so did Satan, leaning over at
such an angle Daniel had to stand in the stirrups to
keep himself mounted. Satan then positioned himself between the calf and the cow.

The calf started to swerve away towards some
heavy brush. Daniel, sensing it was his turn to act,
released his *riata* from the leather retaining thong
hanging from his saddle and, swinging the loop in
the air over his head, released it in the direction
of the calf. More by luck than judgement, it fell over
the calf's head. Daniel wrapped the other end of the
rope round the saddlehorn. The calf, feeling
the noose about its neck, backed up to loosen it.
Satan reacted by walking backwards, keeping the
rope taut and the loop tight.

'Well done, Daniel,' Matt praised him as he rode up. 'You've cut your first dogie.'

'Satan did most of it,' Daniel admitted.

'That's th' way it should be. Th' horse does th' thinkin' an' cuttin' an' you do th' ropin'. Now we goin' to throw that calf.'

Matt took the rope and pulled the calf towards him, at the same time walking towards it. For a moment, the calf just stood there; then it started to try to run. Matt jammed his heels in the dust and pulled. Finally, the calf stood before him.

'Now, you pay 'ttention, Daniel. It ain't hard but you need t' know th' knack.'

Matt put his arm round the calf's neck, put his hand under its jaw, thrust its body against his leg, twisted its head round and back and the animal fell over on its side. Whipping a short length of cord from his belt, Matt hog-tied the animal's four hooves together. Away in the brush, the mother cow bellowed desolately for her offspring.

Beto and Fredo came running, Beto carrying the metal rod which was now red-hot at one end where the metal was shaped into a triangle with a cross in it, Matt's brand. Pressing the searing metal against the animal's rump, a cloud of smoke rose from it, smelling of burnt hair and flesh. As Beto branded the calf, Fredo felt between the calf's hind legs and, pulling its testicles clear, castrated it with several deft cuts with a small knife, the blade sickle-shaped from years of honing. From his pocket he produced a handful of ash and scattered it over the wound.

'Keep off th' flies,' he explained to Daniel, who watched all this with his mouth open in wonderment, 'an' make th' new blood hard quick.'

Matt stood up, slipping the knot that hog-tied the calf's hooves. It struggled with panic to its feet and fled off in the direction of its mother.

'Well don't jus' stan' there like a big ol' bass suckin' at th' surface of th' pond,' he said to Daniel. 'Go git 'nother. An' this time, you're th' one t' throw 'im.'

By midday, all the calves had been branded, the bulls amongst them castrated. The rest of the cattle were then driven out of the stock pen and wandered off into the brush once more, most of them heading at a loping trot for a shallow lake of water half a mile away. Daniel and the others, with the exception of Beto, sat or sprawled under the expansive shadow of a live oak. The sun, pricking through the branches, was hot and the air sultry. Grasshoppers hizzed in the undergrowth while small, nondescript butterflies flitted by on the wing. From a wild hive in a hole high up in the tree came the muted hum of bees.

'You're a real *vaquero* now, boy!' No-Head exclaimed to Daniel, easing his spine against the gnarled tree trunk and tugging his hat down low over his brow.

Daniel made no reply. His spine ached, his legs were so tired he felt he would hardly be able to stand, let alone mount Satan, who was resting in the shade of another vast live oak with the other horses. Trinity had just finished watering them and they stood unmoving except for the flick of a tail.

Beto, who had been busy over by the fire, approached with a tin plate piled high with pieces of meat that looked like fire-blackened cauliflower florets. He handed the plate round. Each man took one and, dunking it in a chilli and vinegar sauce in a mug on the edge of the place, ate it with relish.

'What is it?' Daniel enquired as the plate reached him.

'Prairie oysters,' No-Head said.

Daniel chose a piece, dipping it in the spicy sauce and biting into it. It was delicious, as soft as fish but grainy and unlike any meat he had ever eaten.

'Oysters?' Daniel repeated. 'But we're over a hundred miles from the sea.'

'*Señorito*,' Fredo said, grinning. 'Is not a real oyster. Is' – he put his hand between his legs – 'the pieces of the bull calves I cut.'

Early one morning, just as Daniel was waking, Matt came into the bunkhouse and picked up his hat from the end of his bunk.

'Now this,' he said contemptuously as he held it up, 'ain't a hat. It's a derby. How're you to catch a drink with this?'

Daniel looked bemused.

Matt beckoned to him. Daniel followed him to the water trough where the rancher took off his Stetson, dipped the wide brim in the water and put it to his lips. Water ran down his chin, wetting his shirt, but he still took in enough to quench a thirst.

'Now that's a hat,' Matt remarked, putting it back on his head and wiping his chin on his sleeve, 'an' we've to fix you up with one.' He handed Daniel his hat back and became more serious. 'Daniel,' he began, 'I have to be honest. When I first set eyes on you I thought you was sure to be a waste of breathin' air. Molly was all for keepin' you jus' for th' chores an' if you run off, then what th' hell! Jus' so long as you didn't run off with nothin' that weren't yours. But, since then, you've proved yourself a baby buckaroo an' no mistake. So, seein' as you has no money of your own, I'm fittin' you out. Tomorrow, you an' me're goin' for a ride.'

True to his word, just after dawn the following day, Matt and Daniel rode away from Dark Creek, side by side. By the late afternoon, the sun scorching down, they approached a small river, a sluggish stream of emerald-green water the banks of which were thickly lined with bushes and trees. Matt reined his horse in behind a bush-covered hillock two hundred yards from the treeline. Dismounting, he tethered the animal to a fallen mesquite trunk and indicated Daniel do the same with Satan. Then, at a crouch, they moved up the hillock until they could just see through the bushes to the riverine trees.

'Always remember this, Daniel,' Matt murmured. 'Trees an' water make for danger. If someone was to ambush us, this'd be th' place. They got cover; we're in th' open. They're low down, we're outlined 'gainst th' sky. Th' minute we move, we're as plain t' see as a sally in a shootin' stall at th' fair.'

As he spoke, he studied the trees.

'Can you see anyone?' Daniel whispered.

'I ain't lookin' for people. You'll not see them. I'm lookin' for signs,' Matt replied.

'Signs?' Daniel echoed.

'A scared bird flying off. A road runner dashin' away. Maybe a white-tail deer snortin'. Th' snuffle of a horse. Insects an' birds fallin' silent. Signs not all's right.'

A dove flew out of the trees, circled over their heads and settled back from where it came.

'That dove . . .' Daniel began.

'Well,' Matt replied, 'you're learnin'. But that only means there ain't no white man down there. If there was, that dove would've took off way over yonder. Might be an Indian or two, though. They're cunnin' as a hungry coyote.'

Deeming it to be safe, Matt mounted his horse and removed the Spencer rifle from its saddle scabbard, levering a cartridge into the breech and holding it across his chest. Slowly, he and Daniel rode towards the river. In the shade of the trees, the ground was covered in short grass growing between low boulders. Matt rode a hundred yards up and down river in each direction. When he returned, he swung himself out of the saddle, his horse already head down and nibbling at the grass. Daniel dismounted from Satan and started to unbuckle the saddle girth.

'Leave ol' Satan saddled,' Matt advised. 'Never know when you'll need t' make a dash for it.' He looked around. 'We'll settle here th' night.'

By darkness, they had a fire burning brightly between two boulders, a pot of coffee on the boil and a dish of bacon and beans simmering. Daniel lay on his back with his head against a tussock of grass. Overhead, the low flames of the fire flickered on the tree boughs. For a while, neither of them spoke. An owl called persistently some way downriver. Matt ladled some food onto Daniel's plate and handed him a chunk of bread.

'You like it here with us, Daniel?' Matt asked, finally breaking the silence.

'Yes,' Daniel answered, after a pause. 'Yes, I do.'

'An' you got plans, Daniel?'

Daniel pondered this question. Yes, he considered, he had a plan but he wondered if he dared speak of it.

'I'd like to stay and work for you,' he replied at length.

Matt squatted by the fire and poured himself another mug of coffee. 'See, Daniel, Molly an' me'd like another baby, but Molly ... Well, she had a rough time with Trinity and the doctor says . . .' Matt peered into the darkness, the glimmer of the red embers and the occasional small flame picking out his features and glinting on the dull steel of his

Navy Colt. 'I always fancied me a son but it ain't to be. Leastways,' he added pensively, 'not natural wise.'

As Matt finished, Daniel realized why he had not just been taken in by the Gravitts but also given a horse and taught how to shoot the Spencer rifle.

'We'd best get our heads down,' Matt suggested. 'We's a long ride tomorrow.'

No sooner had he spoken than, somewhere nearby, a twig snapped. Instantly, Matt had the Navy Colt out its holster and cocked.

'Keep low,' he hissed.

Another twig cracked.

Matt kicked some earth into the fire, the flames immediately dying down. A thin column of smoke rose into the night sky.

'Evenin', neighbour,' a voice called from out in the darkness.

'Show yourself real slow,' Matt called back.

Gradually, a man materialized from the night.

'State your business, pilgrim,' Matt demanded.

'Cup o' that coffee wouldn't go amiss,' came the reply. 'I smelled it a way off.'

The man walked forwards. He was wearing a long oilskin coat and his spurs clicked with each step.

'Leave your hands where I can see both of 'em,' Matt ordered.

Obeying, the man stepped forwards and lowered himself to the ground by the fire. Daniel put another length of dead mesquite wood on the embers where it quickly ignited, the new flames glancing off the tree trunks and the smoke dying down.

'Ain't you Mr Gravitt of Dark Creek?' the man asked.

'Maybe,' Matt replied. 'What of it?'

The man offered his hand. 'I'm Chas. Chas Davis. Got me a small parcel o' land 'bout halfway t' Laredo. Ain't nothing special.'

'Where's your horse?' Matt enquired, suspiciously.

Davis snapped his fingers three times in quick succession. There was a shifting sound in the darkness and a bay horse entered the ring of firelight.

'Where you headed?' Matt enquired.

'Going back. Been up t' San Antone with twenty head.'

Matt uncocked the Colt and put it back in its holster by his roll. Daniel rinsed his mug out and filled it with coffee, passing it to their guest.

'Sold 'em for twenty dollars a head,' Davis continued. 'Twenty bucks a steer! And they wasn't even that meaty, to tell th' truth.' He looked at Daniel and, taking the mug, nodded his thanks. 'This your boy?'

'In a manner of speakin',' Matt replied, smiling briefly at Daniel. He went on, 'Twenty dollars's a fine price.'

'Things goin' crazy,' Davis said. 'Th' Army's buyin' all th' beef it can get.'

'Th' army?' Matt repeated.

Davis leaned his back against a boulder. 'There's a war buildin', an' when there's a war there's soljers an' them soljers gotta eat an' I guess they like prime rib. Leastways, th' officers do. Th' rest get jerky. No difference. Not to the likes o' you an' me. Still beef . . .'

At daybreak, Matt and Daniel rinsed their faces

in the river. The water was cold and smelled of dead leaves. Refreshed, they mounted their horses and left Davis asleep, snoring with his head against a boulder.

They rode at a steady trot for over an hour. The sun came up, the chill air warming within minutes. It was then Matt reined his horse in to a walk, letting it go at its own speed along the trackway they were following. He made no attempt to speak and it was some time before Daniel dared to ask him what was on his mind.

They travelled at least fifty yards before Matt ventured a reply.

'Well, Daniel,' he said finally, 'I've been reckonin'. If steers're fetching top dollar right now in San Antone, they'll make a deal more than that a head two months from now.'

It had not rained in weeks and a pall of dust hung over the town of San Antonio. Daniel and Matt found a livery stable and left their horses with the ostler before heading for a saloon.

It was a two-storey wooden building, the porch

raised above the level of the dusty street. A number of horses were tethered to a rail before it whilst behind it ran the sluggish waters of the San Antonio River, the banks lined by reeds. Here and there, rickety wooden footbridges spanned it. Matt pushed the saloon door open and entered. Daniel followed him.

The interior was dark and cool after the heat of the day, the air smelling of beer, whiskey and sweat. A long bar ran the length of the room. Behind it stood a bar-keep in a black-and-silver embroidered waistcoat, his shirtsleeves rolled up to the elbow and held back by a black ribbon. Above his head hung a notice which read NO DANCING ON THE TABLES IN SPURS. A staircase on one side rose to a gallery leading off which were a number of doors. At scrubbed wooden tables men sat drinking or playing cards but most leaned against the bar, deep in animated conversation. Matt and Daniel joined them.

'What's all th' agitation about?' Matt asked the bar-keep as he ordered a beer for himself and a sarsaparilla for Daniel.

'You ain't heard, sir?' He pushed a tankard of beer across the counter. 'Union troops've killed innocent folk in St. Louis. Now th' talk's all of fightin'.'

'You damn' right, 'keep!' exclaimed a man standing next to Matt. He was wearing a dented billy-cock hat and a dusty coat frayed at the cuffs. 'The North wants to free all th' slaves. We got no choice but t' defend our rights 'gainst them ig'orant northerners.'

'We have to cut down them Stars 'n' Bars!' said another. 'Join round our flag.'

'Them fancy northern folks,' a third man butted in, 'jus' don't unnerstand how we's livin'. They jus' don't get it that there ain't no cotton if there ain't no slaves.'

'Tryin' to destroy us, they are,' remarked yet another. 'Take our land. Starve us like we was vermin . . .'

Matt sipped his beer, the froth gathering on his top lip. He wiped it away with his sleeve and said, 'Looks like that's th' way it'll be . . .'

Their drinks consumed, Matt led Daniel out of

the saloon and down the street to a shop over the front of which hung a sign reading PARIS HATTERS. They entered to be met by a tall, strongly built man with wavy grey hair wearing a black waistcoat covered in felt dust.

'I can see what your need is,' the hat maker said, running an eye up and down Daniel's clothes. 'That boy's hat's 'bout as much use as an umbrella in a twister.'

It took fifteen minutes to shape a hat to fit Daniel's head. He watched as an assistant steamed the felt, shaping and cutting it, bending it to fit him. Finally, the assistant brushed the hat and gave it to Daniel. It fitted snugly, with a broad brim and a flat crown.

'I calls that th' gambler's style,' the hat maker announced. 'Same as them riverboat card sharps wear. You make sure you ain't taken for one of them bunko steerers.'

Leaving the hatter's, Matt took Daniel into a gunsmith's. As they entered, a bell chimed tinnily over the door and the gunsmith appeared through a door at the rear.

'Can I be of help, sir?' he enquired, rubbing his hands on a cloth apron besmirched with gun oil.

'I want a Navy Colt,' Matt replied. 'Five hundred rounds. Holster, belt. Make th' belt short.'

'For a lady, sir?'

'No,' Matt answered, looking at Daniel. 'For him.'

The gunsmith took a pistol down from a rack behind the counter, polishing it with an oily rag. From beneath the counter, he produced ten fawn-coloured cardboard boxes with blue labels and handed the revolver to Matt, who passed it to Daniel.

'That's a mighty big gun for a little boy,' the gunsmith remarked patronizingly.

'No, sir,' Matt replied. 'It's a mighty big gun for a little man.'

They arrived back at Dark Creek just before night-fall on the following day, spending the intervening night camping on the Nueces River once again, but at a different location. It was Matt's decision never to camp in the same spot twice. That, he declared, was to invite trouble.

Chapter 4

★

LEAVIN'
DARK CREEK

Matt said little throughout the evening meal. Only when Beto or No-Head addressed him directly about matters concerning the ranch or the livestock did he speak and, even then, his replies were short and succinct. It was not until Molly produced an apple pie that he cleared his throat and addressed everyone.

'I've somethin' t' say t' y'all,' he began portentously.

Molly started to cut into the pie. The aroma

of baked apples and cinnamon filled the air.

'I've done me some thinkin',' Matt went on, 'and I can't jus' sit back whilst those Blue Bellies overrun th' South. As y'all know, Texas has joined th' Confederacy of Southern States. Now we has to stand up for our rights.'

'Why're they 'gainst us?' Trinity asked, a little puzzled. 'Th' Blue Bellies protected us from th' Comanches and Apaches and th' Mexican *banditos* an' all an' now they're gunnin' for us.'

'They want to set th' slaves free,' Matt explained. 'Yet, if they do that, th' farmers'll go down. How can they work their land if they don't have negras to till th' soil an' pick th' cotton?'

'We don't have slaves,' Molly observed as she cut the last slice of pie. 'We pay our *vaqueros*. Th' cotton farmers'll jus' have to do th' same's us with their slaves.'

'It's not that simple,' Matt responded.

'Simple's got nothin' to do with it,' May-Anne cut in, refusing a piece of the pie. 'Keepin' slaves is wrong. No man ought to own another. I've heard talk that ownin' a slave's no diff'rent from ownin' a horse. No way how you looks at it, a horse ain't a man and vice versa.'

'Be that as it may,' Matt continued. 'The North's our enemy now an' . . .'

'An'?' Molly asked.

'An' I've got to do my share. Jus' like when Santa Anna attacked Texas. Men rallied to th' fight. Men from all over. Bill Travis, Jim Bowie, Davy Crockett.'

'An' they died,' Molly said bluntly. 'You've just come back from San Antone. You've seen th' Alamo. You know what happened. Whole bunch of 'em was massacred. Didn't even get a Christian burial. They burned all of 'em on a bonfire. Weren't no different from burning diseased hogs.'

'This time, it's not—' Matt started, but his wife cut him short.

'Matt Gravitt,' Molly said, 'it don't matter how godly or not was th' man who pulled th' trigger. A bullet's still a bullet no matter th' cause it's fired for.'

'I have to go,' Matt insisted softly. 'I'm a Texan an' it's my duty. I'll not have others die for me when

71

I've not played my part. Besides, it might be slavery now that the Blue Bellies're out to stop, but what's next?'

Everyone round the table fell silent.

'And, pray tell, what happens to Dark Creek whilst you're away fightin' for rights you don't exercise anyway?' Molly asked caustically.

'I've thought of that an' I have a plan,' Matt answered. 'Fredo an' Miguel take charge under you, Molly. We bring in a few more *vaqueros* to help 'em out – you know some good men, Fredo?'

'*Si, señor!* My two brothers. They are work hard. In Mexico, they are *vaqueros*. Also, *señor*, Miguel's – how you say? – mother's brother's son—'

'Cousin,' No-Head interrupted, adding, 'But how 'bout me? You don't reckon I'm up to th' task? I been workin' here with y'all—'

'I reckon you're good. Real good,' Matt cut in. ''s why I got other plans for you. This war's pushin' up th' price of beef. So you, Beto, Daniel and my little girl here' – he put his hand on Trinity's shoulder – ''re goin' on a cattle drive t' make us a pocket o' money. Beto, you fetch along your friend, Jesus. I

72

hear tell he's more than handy with a cookin' pot.'

'I don't want you t' go off t' th' war . . .' Molly began.

'Neither do I want t' go, dear bride,' Matt stopped her, putting his arm around her waist and drawing her in to his side, kissing her on the cheek. 'This war's going t' be meaner than a blue norther. Men'll die, sure as snow melts in th' desert. But it ain't goin' t' last long. Four months, I reckon, and it'll all be over. It'll be nothin' more than a summer storm . . .'

Molly gave her husband an askance glance of disbelief.

For the next three days, Daniel and Beto were kept busy rounding up the cattle and, at No-Head's command, cutting out those animals for the journey north and driving them into the corral near the ranch house. Once the cattle were in, Daniel and Trinity were set the job of keeping them watered and fed.

'Have you done this before?' Daniel enquired of Trinity as they pitchforked fodder together over the corral fence-rail.

'Oh, sure!' Trinity exclaimed. 'Every winter, it's been my chore if we have some weak dogies in here as needs fattenin'.'

'No,' Daniel said. 'I mean, driven cattle.'

'Sure I done it b'fore,' Trinity responded off-handedly. 'I drove half a dozen to San Antone one time and twenty head to Laredo another.' She leaned on her pitchfork and looked Daniel up and down. He felt as if, for the first time, she was really noticing him. 'You're not scared, are you?'

Daniel decided there was nothing to be gained by prevaricating and replied, 'Yes. I'm scared. I know nothing about driving cattle. It's been only weeks since I learned how to cut one.'

The sunlight glared off the dusty soil. Trinity removed her hat, slapped the dust out of it, put it back on and squinted at him.

'You ain't afraid t' admit you're scared?'

'No,' Daniel said. 'It's the truth. There's no point in hiding it.'

'Truth be told, I got my doubts,' Trinity admitted. 'But don't you go say nothin' t' nobody.'

Daniel smiled to himself. Trinity was, he now

realized, like him. For all her toughness she had her doubts and fears, just like he did.

'You ain't laughin' at me, are you, boy?' she rounded on him.

'No,' Daniel replied. 'I'm not laughing at you.'

He tossed another load of fodder over the rail, the cattle quick to start pulling at it, their mouths chewing from side to side.

'I'll look out for you if you look out for me,' he continued.

'You got a deal,' Trinity answered and she thrust her fork into the fodder pile.

When he was not caring for the steers, Daniel went some way off into the brush and practised with the Navy Colt, shooting at flat stones balanced on a tree stump. Whenever he hit one, the stone shattered, the bullet whining off into the air like a squalling, irate tomcat. After two days and four boxes of ammunition, he reasoned he was as proficient as he would ever be, hitting the stone four times out of six.

For a week, Dark Creek Ranch was in a state of

organized turmoil. Molly spent her time sewing patches on Matt's clothing because, she reasoned, a soldier was going to live rough and fight hard and his clothes would take, as she put it, 'th' brunt of the wearin''. Trinity was engaged in cooking cakes of pemmican whilst Beto was employed in making a stout leather satchel for Matt to carry his kit in. Daniel gave Matt's tackle several applications of dubbin until the leather was as smooth and as supple – and as waterproof – as was possible. Matt kept himself busy drawing maps and charts, cleaning his Navy Colt and cutting his initials carefully into the wooden stock of one of the Spencer rifles. Even May-Anne, as she suckled her baby, whose name had by now been shortened to Tad, gave what help she could by stirring pots or sewing.

Finally, the night before he was to set out for San Antonio to enlist, Matt took Daniel, Trinity, No-Head and Beto aside and sat them down round the ranch-house table.

'Now, see here,' Matt started, 'I've been puttin' my mind t' this an' I reckon th' best place f' us t' shift some beeves is up north in Kansas City.'

'Why do we have to go all th' way t' Kansas City, Papa?' Trinity questioned her father. 'Why can't we jus' go t' San Antone an' sell the steers there? We done it before.'

'B'cause, my sweet child,' Matt replied, 'th' price'll be higher there. There's a mess o' mil'tary activity up there an' I heard talk in San Antone there's a real need for beeves. Kansas City's waverin'. Sometimes it's for the Confederation, sometimes it's for the North. Our troops there'll need a bolsterin'. You can be sure they ain't nec'ssarily gettin' a load o' co-operation from the locals.'

'And the best way to give an army victory is to keep its stomach full,' Daniel commented.

'You're damn' right, Daniel!' Matt exclaimed.

'That'll do for cussin', Matt Gravitt!' Molly rebuked her husband. 'Save that talk for your soldier friends.'

'Anyways, I've prepared some maps for you,' Matt continued. 'They ain't too acc'rate but they's th' best I can do. Been some time since I was up that way.' He spread out some sheets of paper with his hands. 'This first is a map from San Antone to th' Red River. Make sure you pass Fort Worth well to th' east. No way of tellin' who's got th' garrison. Us or th' Blue Bellies. I've been mullin' over where it's best t' cross th' river an' I reckon it's just a mile or so east of Mound City. Don't you get no ideas, though. This ain't no city. No, sir! This is nothin' more than a bundle of sticks tied together to make a house or two. There's a riverboat jetty nearby, an' that's 'bout it.' He pointed to the map. 'See here, th' river's real narrow. Take 'em 'cross upstream from th' narrow an' you can swim 'em over. Even if th' river's high an' runnin', it ain't too much for th' steers. This time of year, th' water should be low but you watch for flash floods. Keep an eye out for thunderheads droppin' rain. In Mound City – 'bout th' entire population, I'd say – is a man called R. T. Bryarly. He'll advise you on what to find 'cross th' river. Once you're over th' water, you're in th' Indian Territories which some folks call No-man's Land.

'On th' subject of Indians,' Matt continued, 'a year or two back, there was a lot of fightin' between Anglos and th' Comanches in th' western side of th'

Indian Territories. Died down now, they say, but you never know. As if that ain't enough, two tribes called th' Caddoes and th' Wacoes've been moved by th' gov'ment into th' Indian Territories which may've unsettled th' other tribes.'

He paused and unfolded a second map.

'Anyways, over th' river y'll then clamp eyes on th' Ouachita Mountains. T' get through 'em's easy 'nough. Jus' head more or less due north, keepin' t' any valley or pass that runs north–south. In time, y'all hit th' Canadian River. T' hold on t' th' right direction . . .' He felt in his pocket, taking out a brass-cased pocket compass and handing it to Daniel. 'You know how t' use one o' these?'

'Yes,' Daniel replied.

'Then you'll take charge of th' navigation, Daniel. I reckon if you can find your way here from London, then sure as snakes bite you can find th' way to Kansas City.'

Daniel didn't point out to Matt that when he set out from England he had actually been aiming for Australia. He studied the compass, the brass warm from being in Matt's pocket. It was heavy, the lid opening to give a sight line, the needle within turning on a mother-of-pearl disc, the degrees engraved around the outer rim.

'I'll want that back,' Matt remarked. 'Belonged to my daddy ... He brung that with him from Brownsville. It found him Dark Creek ...' He turned his attention to the second map. 'It ain't an easy route to keep to, passin' up th' eastern side of th' Indian Territories. It might be you encounter Indians but it's not they y'all need to be wary of. That's th' Anglos. Some o' 'em's sure to be for us but some'll be 'gainst us. An' you have to get over th' Canadian River. Now, listen up! Th' best place for that is 'bout sixty miles west of Fort Smith. Th' fort, I hear, ain't a fort no more but that don't mean it ain't still dang'rous. Look f' a trail running east–west alongside th' south bank of th' river. It was made by the Forty-Niners back during the gold rush. Hold t' th' track west till you cross a creek an' th' land starts t' rise. Look for a burial ground. Beyond's a track down to th' river. It's real steep. Guide th' beasts into a gully an' down to th' river and take 'em across to a long thin island, not much

more than a mudbank. Then it's a little way to th'
far shore. River ain't usually fast but it's wide. Once
over th' river, bear jus' east o' north. After a few
days, you'll come to a trail. Cross it then jus' keep
right on t' Kansas City . . .'

'That'll be th' trail from Fort Smith t' Perryman's
trading post?' suggested No-Head.

'Got it in one!' replied Matt. 'Been that way
before, No-Head?'

'A while back,' No-Head confirmed, 'when my
thoughts an' dreams was still more or less open t'
th' sky.'

'How far is it?' Daniel asked.

Matt pondered a moment and said, 'From here t'
Kansas City? Two months or so; 'bout eight
hundred miles.'

No one spoke very much over the evening meal,
each lost in their own thoughts. When it was over,
Matt shook hands with No-Head, Daniel and the
vaqueros.

'Do good by me, y' hear,' he murmured quietly.

They all nodded sombrely but said nothing.

* * *

When Daniel woke from a fitful sleep just before dawn, Matt had already departed.

The day was spent loading the wagon, packing saddle rolls and making certain everyone was ready for their departure. Daniel was amazed by the provisions they were taking: a sack of flour, a side of salted bacon, oatmeal, beans and dried fruit, lard, sugar, rice and coffee, beef jerky and pemmican, salt, pepper, dried fish, pilot bread, crackers, a stone jug of brandy and a bottle of whiskey – 'Medic'nal use only, y'hear,' Molly stressed. In addition were two iron crutches-and-bars for cooking, several lanterns and lamp oil, a barrel of water, rope, ammunition, a small tent and much more.

Around mid-morning, the cattle were driven out of the corral and started off in a line past the ranch house and barns and into the brush. Roja appeared from the bushes behind the barn and jumped onto the wagon. Molly, the *vaqueros* being left behind and May-Anne, baby Tad in her arms, solemnly waved goodbye. One of the *vaqueros* made the sign of the cross on his chest and forehead.

'They look so sad,' Trinity said quietly, sniffing and wiping a single tear from her eye, leaving a dusty smear on her cheek.

'We'll be back,' Daniel said, not so much to comfort Trinity as to reassure himself. This was after all, he thought, a new venture for her; yet, for him, it was nothing more than another stage in his journey. His life . . .

Chapter 5

★

HOW NO-HEAD GOT HIS NAME

In three days, they reached the vicinity of San Antonio. While Beto and Trinity kept with the herd, No-Head, Daniel and Jesus paid a quick visit to the town to buy more supplies – lucifers, two more gallons of lamp oil, additional lengths of rope, another small stone jug of whiskey and, at No-Head's insistence, two brand-new Spencer rifles with five hundred rounds of ammunition.

'If we's likely t' fetch us a bit of trouble . . .' he remarked, handing one of the rifles to Daniel and returning their money pouch to a small strongbox in a hidden compartment in the camp wagon. 'I don't reckon that's a waste of our resources. 'Sides, Matt gave me permission t' buy us a bit more fire power.'

On the fourth day out of San Antonio, they reached the state capital of Austin, crossing the Colorado River on a wooden bridge which swayed precariously under the passage of the steers. The streets and avenues were lined with elegant buildings behind neat gardens contained within white-painted picket fences. Here and there, well-dressed gentlemen walked along wide sidewalks, ladies on their arms. Somewhere in the town, a church bell tolled.

As the last steer reached the northern end of the bridge, a man approached them on horseback. He was wearing black trousers with a gold stripe down the side, and his grey double-breasted jacket was tight-fitting, with gold braid on the sleeves, two rows of brass buttons and a line of gold piping. On the collar were two gold bars of braid and a yellow flash. His slouch hat was black with a crossed swords insignia in gold braid and a braid ribbon hatband.

Reining his horse in between Daniel and Trinity, he saluted smartly and said, 'You cow-pokes sure could do with a dip in th' river.'

'We aren't cow-pokes, sir,' Daniel replied tartly, stung by the remark. 'We're *vaqueros*.'

The man laughed loudly and said, 'Indeed! Well, I reckon you're right, young sir. At least you got this far.'

Daniel was about to bridle when the man removed his hat. For a moment, neither Daniel nor Trinity spoke then, almost dubiously, Trinity said, 'Papa?'

Matt grinned and replied, 'You're lookin' at Cavalry Major Matthew Gravitt of the Army of the Confederacy. They made me an officer right off. But,' he added, his voice softening, 'I'm still your ol' daddy.'

Matt rode with them for a few miles. Here and there, they met other men on horseback who saluted, even though they were not in uniform. Two ladies passed by in a buggy driven by a negro in livery and a top hat. They waved coyly, the lace frills on their cream silk parasols flapping in the breeze. In a vegetable field, a line of black men tilled the soil, stripped to the waist and singing together in low tones as they swung their hoes.

''re those slaves?' Trinity asked Daniel.

'I think so,' he replied but Matt, overhearing the question, added, 'They're slaves, right 'nough. A third of the city's population is slaves.'

'Why're they after freein' 'em?' Trinity wondered aloud. 'They don't look so unhappy.'

'It ain't t' do with happiness,' Matt answered. 'It's t' do with politics.'

Three miles north of Austin, Matt left them, giving Trinity, then Daniel, a hug.

'You take care of yourselves, y'hear? If I come back safe from the war, I don't want t' find one of you was bit by a rattler, drownded in a flood nor struck by lightning nor nothin'.'

With that he saluted, waved and turned his horse, heading back the way they had come at a gallop. Roja ran after him for a hundred yards or so, then stopped and returned to the wagon.

'You sure is one lazy hound,' No-Head remarked. 'A real tenderpaw.'

As Matt disappeared, the sound of his horse's hooves fading, one word of his stuck in Daniel's mind. It was not *rattler* nor was it *lightning* nor *flood*. It was *if*.

For the first ten miles or so, they had to keep the cattle on the trail. To either side were farmsteads or orchards of saplings, protected from passing cattle by stout fences. Gradually, however, these settlements gave way to virgin brush and grassland.

The way in which the steers were driven was not what Daniel had expected. He had thought they would be kept in a bunch and made to trot but in fact quite the opposite occurred. They sauntered along at a walk, strung out in a line over fifty yards wide. They held their heads low down and made no sound except for the monotonous plod of their hooves. At the front of this straggling column rode Beto. Behind him came the lead steer. Daniel had not known how it had happened, but the steers seemed to have elected one of their number to be their guide. Every so often, the riders changed places, Beto dropping to take up the rear and someone else leading the boss steer. This way, everyone took turns at, as No-Head put it, 'eatin' th' trail', by which he meant breathing in the dust kicked up by the steers. When not leading or taking up the rearguard position, the other two riders made their way up and down the column, making sure no animal ambled off into the brush to be lost.

At midday, the column halted. Jesus, who was driving the camp wagon some way to the rear beyond the dust cloud, caught up with the rest and quickly prepared a fire over which he brewed a pot of coffee and heated a pan of beans. Then they all sat or squatted in the shade of the wagon. The steers wandered off into the brush to find some shade or fodder. The horses were tethered under a mesquite tree.

'When do we go on?' Daniel asked. It seemed to him they were making very slow progress.

'First,' Beto said, 'we have a *siesta*. Not just us, but the horses and steers also. They must get used to much walking.' He lay on the ground, put his sombrero over his face and was soon snoring lightly.

Daniel lay on his side under the wagon, his feet protruding out into the sunlight, his head resting on his arm as a pillow. He dozed for half an hour, listening to the birds and insects in the brush. When he came to, the first thing he saw once his eyes had adjusted to the sunlight, was something moving on the ground close to his face. In all about six inches long, it looked like a creature from his worst nightmare, a cross between a lizard and a bloated frog, mottled sand in colour with bowed legs ending in clawed toes and a long tail. Its head was covered in grotesque spikes and spines. It might, he thought, have been created out of a cactus. For a moment he thought he was dreaming. Suddenly, the creature bloated itself up and hissed ominously.

Letting out a yelp, Daniel sat bolt upright and banged his head on the underside of the wagon; he frantically scrabbled to get clear of the creature. Trinity jumped down from the wagon, her boots thumping on the ground.

'He ain't likely t' do you no damage,' she declared when she saw this miniature monster.

The creature ran a few feet then flattened itself against the dry soil under a thorny shrub, its mottled markings darkening in the shade.

'What is it?' Daniel asked, the hairs on the back of his neck still prickling, his arms bumped with goose-pimples.

'Jus' an ol' horn'd toad,' Trinity told him. ''s not really a toad but a lizard. Don't bite. Ain't pois'nous. You get him riled, he jus' puffs up and tries to make somethin' of himself.'

Daniel smirked sheepishly, rubbed the growing bump on his head and brushed the dust off his clothes. The horned toad, after waiting a moment, streaked away.

'Boy!' Trinity remarked. 'You really has a lot t' learn.'

'You think I don't know?' Daniel retorted ironically.

'I was jus' sayin',' Trinity came back.

Eventually, the *siesta* came to an end. Jesus extinguished the fire, everyone mounted up, rounded up the cattle, which had not strayed far, counted them to ensure none were missing and once more headed north.

As the sun was nearing the horizon, they reached a small creek. No-Head decreed that this was where they would stop for the night. The cattle and horses drank their fill and Jesus once again lit a fire on which he heated another pot of coffee and prepared tortilla soup in a small, smoke-blackened iron cauldron. While the food was simmering, he erected a small tent for Trinity next to the camp wagon.

Just after nightfall, a white sickle moon rose, thin as an eyelash upon the black sky. Daniel lay on his back in his bedroll, his saddle acting as a pillow. In imitation of No-Head and Beto, he slept with his Navy Colt beside his head, loaded but not cocked. Alone in himself, his thoughts mulled over the past few days.

Daniel realized he had indeed learned a great deal since leaving Dark Creek. Apart from the embarrassing episode with the horned toad, he was now wiser by far in the ways of the *vaquero*. For one, a cattle drive seemed to him to be a leisurely matter. It did not so much involve driving the cattle as keeping them steadily on the move in the general direction required. The lead steer seemed to follow the front rider's horse by instinct. If a steer wandered off at a tangent, to investigate a tasty-looking bush or patch of grass, it usually rejoined the main column without even so much as a prod; the mere appearance of Daniel and Satan was sufficient to turn it. To encourage the herd to keep going, No-Head and Beto occasionally called out to them.

'Move along! Hey-ey-ey-ey-ey! Git there! Hyip-hyip!'

Trinity keened at them. Daniel took to whistling or imitating the men. He tried keening, but it hurt his throat. He also learnt how to ride for hours on end without his muscles seizing up. Beto taught him.

'Is simple, *señorito*,' he said. 'Preten' you are a piece of th' horse. If he move one way, you move one way. Is like a dance with beautiful woman. You . . .' He moved his hand in the air as if conducting an invisible and silent orchestra playing a lullaby.

Daniel tried it. It worked. Within half an hour, his aching muscles were relaxed and he felt strangely calm, as if Satan's motion was rocking him into semi-consciousness. The broad, comfortable saddle with its high rear edge helped, giving support to his lumbar muscles.

Driving the steers required more than just maintaining a steady walking pace. It also entailed keeping an eye on them, watching to see if one was sick, another lame. The former might spread disease to the others, the latter slow them up. To accommodate them, the sick could be dosed with medicinal herbs from a bag Jesus carried in the camp wagon, the pace of the drive slackened to allow the lame to recover.

Furthermore, in addition to driving the cattle, there were other chores to be done. One of these was to acquire meat for the pot. This task was given to Daniel, who would ride out into the brush for a mile or so, armed with a double-barrelled shotgun kept in the camp wagon. Once there, Daniel let Satan walk slowly through the brush while he searched for suitable prey. Most days, he returned with a dozen quail, a few cottontails or jack rabbits. One day, by sheer chance, he came upon some wild turkeys feeding in a clearing and succeeded in downing two with a left and a right. At the first shot, the whole flock took to the air, squawking and gobbling with indignation and alarm. The second bird Daniel took on the wing. It was not a difficult shot. The turkeys were large birds and clumsy flyers.

The most dangerous task was scouting ahead. Not only had a way to be found through the brush but one had to keep alert for signs of Indians and other humans. Daniel only rode point, as No-Head put it, when there was no perceived risk of meeting other people, yet the possibility of attack was always present. The Indians would want the horses and the others the cattle.

After a week, Daniel felt himself to be an experienced *vaquero*, yet, one evening, it was brought home to him just how much he still had to learn.

They had stopped for the night. Jesus was butchering a jack rabbit, Trinity baking tortillas on a flat iron griddle. Beto was sitting by the fire but No-Head was twenty yards away by a creek that was little more than a chain of puddles muddied by the cattle and horses drinking. He had undressed to his long-johns and was squatting by a rock at the water's edge. Daniel watched him. He took a handful of wet sand and rubbed it into his shirt: then, taking a stone, he hit the seams hard with it, rubbing the sand in between blows. When he had done the shirt, he started on his trousers. Daniel scratched his stomach where some insect had bitten him and, standing, went down to the creek.

'What're you doing?' he asked.

'Pants rats!' No-Head exclaimed.

'What?' Daniel said, not sure if he had heard correctly.

'Pants rats,' came the reply. 'Seam squirrels. I seed you scratchin' your belly jus' now like you was an ol' flead'd hound. You got 'em, too.' No-Head looked up and saw that Daniel had no idea what he was talking about. 'A pants rat's a louse,' he explained. 'You get all sweaty an' th' dust an' th' steers and th' lack of a laundry bucket . . .' He worked more sand into the seams of his trousers. 'Th' sand's all rough an' scrunches 'em up. Th' ones th' sand don't get the stone do.' He hammered all down the seam. 'You'd best do your clothes. If they itch an' you scratch, th' wound can go septic real quick. An' they can give you a real bad fever. Then you're no more use 'n a two-legged stool. Might just as well be shot.'

Daniel removed his shirt then looked up towards the camp wagon. He had no underwear. If he took his pants off, he would be naked in front of Trinity. No-Head read his thoughts.

'You take 'em off,' he advised. 'You ain't got nothin' she ain't seed before.' He turned and called, 'Miss Trinity, you keep your eyes averted now. Daniel here's goin' huntin'.'

Yet Daniel was still embarrassed.

'Give me that shirt here,' No-Head commanded.

Daniel handed his shirt over. No-Head ran his horny thumbnail down one of the seams and held his hand out to Daniel. Upon his nail was collected a greyish-white mass. Daniel peered closely. It was moving and made up of tiny, insect-like animals about one tenth of an inch long.

'Them's pants rats,' No-Head said. 'See them black bits in their bodies? That's your blood they've been an' swallered.'

With no further thought for Trinity, Daniel quickly removed his trousers and set about with damp sand and a stone to de-louse his clothing.

'See,' No-Head went on to explain, 'it don't matter how much you wash yourself. You can be bright as a new pin, clean as a gold watch, th' pants rats is still there 'cos of th' fact they live on your clothes, not on you. Fact is, they like a clean skin to suck on.'

Over the next two days, the going became more and more difficult. The vegetation grew thicker until it was little less than a high, impenetrable wall of thorny foliage.

'Know what they say 'bout Texas?' No-Head asked Daniel, sardonically. 'If it don't sting, it bites an' if it don't bite or sting, it pricks.'

With that, he rode off to find high ground, returning an hour later.

'We got us a problem,' he declared as he swung down from his saddle, 'but it ain't so bad as I had a mind it was. This chaparral only goes on for a mile or two.' He turned to Beto. 'I say we call a halt here.

Let th' steers get their wind and fill their bellies. Meantime, we cut us a trail through. That way, we can keep th' steers together an' we don't lose 'em or have th' wily ones sneakin' off where we can't see nor find 'em. I don't fancy bein' no brush-poppin' *brasada* buckaroo in that mess of unfrien'ly foliage.'

Beto agreed and the two of them set off with machetes to start hacking at the chaparral. Daniel and Trinity drove the steers to a small swampy area covered in lush grass. Nearby, Jesus set up camp for the night. He soon had a fire going and the usual pot of coffee boiling. Daniel and Trinity rode circle, keeping the herd together. There was little need. Not one steer tried to break from the area of grass. The easy task gave them time to talk.

'Daniel,' Trinity began as their horses came together, 'tell me 'bout Englan'.'

Daniel had to think for a moment. So much had come to pass since he had last set eyes on his homeland. He had seen so many things, visited so many places – coconut palm-lined islands, banana trees, monkeys like little wizened dwarves, seas as high as

99

a house, winds that tore sails as easily as paper, black people, death . . .

'England's like this swamp all over,' he said at last.

'You mean wet an' boggy?' Trinity replied, their horses' hooves sucking at a particularly boggy patch.

'No,' Daniel answered. 'It does rain a great deal but I meant it was like this grass. Rich and green. The trees are green, not sort of dark green like mesquites but bright green, especially in the spring.'

He pictured in his mind his parents' orchard, the boughs laden with pinkish apple blossom, the sheep wandering in emerald grass up to their bellies; and when a breeze ruffled them, the trees dropped a gentle blizzard of petals.

'What are the houses like, Daniel?'

Daniel described the house in which he had lived, which his parents had rented from the local land-lord. He spoke of the thatched roof, the time-blackened timbers, the cob walls and the deep-set windows, the chimney rising at one end. The memory saddened him and he wondered what the house would be like now. Fallen down and neglected, or occupied by a new tenant. The trees, he thought, would have been pruned several times since he had last looked upon them or climbed into their branches to harvest the fruit, making sure he did not grasp an apple hollowed out by wasps or hornets.

'Did you have no brothers nor sisters?'

'I had a sister,' Daniel admitted after a pause, 'but . . .' He left the rest unsaid. Satan knew the truth and that was enough for him.

Trinity reached over and touched Daniel's hand where he was loosely holding the reins.

'Well don't you be of a sorrowful mind,' Trinity said brightly. 'You's a new life now. A new house, new parents.' She smiled coyly. 'New sister.'

As night fell, No-Head and Beto returned. They were hot, caked in sweat and dust, tired but triumphant.

'We ain't got us a way through,' No-Head announced. 'We got us a goldarn highway.'

After they had eaten, Beto took first turn riding circle. They split the night up into four three-hour periods, drawing lots each evening by No-Head tossing a coin. While the others sat around the fire, the flames dying down now the cooking was done, Trinity returned to her quizzing of Daniel.

'You ever see'd th' Queen of Englan'?'

'Queen Victoria?' Daniel replied. 'No. She lives most of the while in London and that was over fifty miles away.'

'So you never been t' Lond'n?' No-Head added.

'I've been twice,' Daniel responded.

Trinity, who had been lying back against one of the wheels of the camp wagon, sat up.

'Tell us 'bout Lond'n!' she exclaimed eagerly. 'I'd jus' love t' go t' Lond'n.'

'It's a big city,' Daniel began.

'As big as Corpus Christi?'

'A hundred times bigger,' Daniel replied.

'That's a load o' bull chips!' No-Head retorted.

'It's the truth,' Daniel affirmed.

He went on to describe the streets packed with hansom cabs and horse-drawn trams, the big squares around which the wealthy resided and the rows of tenements where the less well-off lived,

Trafalgar Square, Westminster Abbey and St Paul's Cathedral, the Tower of London, the busy pubs, the smell of horse dung, ale, smoke and bread baking in an oven.

'Hell's teeth!' No-Head said. 'I'd like t' see me some o' that.'

He poked the embers of the fire with a stick and threw a thick mesquite log onto them, sparks rising into the sky to be extinguished like shooting stars. As soon as the log took flame, Daniel was suddenly hit on the back of the head by something small and hard. He looked round but could see nothing beyond the ring of firelight. It happened again. Then again. Glancing sideways, he saw something strike Trinity's hat and bounce off. It was about the size of a cherry pip.

'Bet they ain't t' be foun' in Lond'n!' No-Head remarked with a grin.

'What are they?' Daniel asked as another hit his neck.

'Bugs,' No-Head responded. 'Beetles. Little critters that eat bull chips. If it weren't for them, th' prairie'd be dog deep in dung.'

103

As they prepared to settle for the night, Trinity nudged Daniel, winked and whispered, 'Ask No-Head how he got 'is name.'

'May I ask you a question?' Daniel asked.

'Sure thing,' No-Head replied.

'What is your real name?'

'Abraham,' No-Head replied. 'Jus' like that pesky pres'dent.'

'So why do they call you No-Head?'

'Same reason as I don't take off my hat.' He answered evasively.

'Why's that?' Daniel persisted.

No-Head came and sat down on the ground beside Daniel and, by the light of the fire, removed his battered hat and tilted his head down so that Daniel could see the top of it. His crown was devoid of hair, which only started sprouting level with his ears below which it was dark brown, collar-length and curly. Not only that, his crown dipped in the middle, the skin in the depression pale white and taut.

'See that little hollow?' No-Head asked. ''bout two inches round? That's where I was scalped by th' Indians.'

'Scalped?' Daniel replied.

'Yup! Sure thing! I was doin' me some fur trappin' up in th' Black Hills. One time, this party of Sioux braves comes across me. They ties me down an' they does a dance an' then one of 'em comes over with a big blade an' he sliced off th' top o' my head as ready as you knock open a boiled egg. Took a piece of th' bone, skin an' my hair.'

Daniel felt his own scalp creep and saw, in his mind's eye, a brief vision of the Karankawa standing between him and the ranch house.

'Lef' me for dead, they did. An' by rights, I should've met th' Lord Almighty right there and then, but this wily ol' prospector came up on me. He fixed th' bleeding an' bound my head and tended me for more'n three months while he panned this stream nearby. End of th' time, he's got near twenty ounces o' gold dust and I got my wits back. Now, I got me a hole in my head big across as a silver dollar.' He pointed at the depression. 'You touch it jus' here, Daniel. Jus' gentle like.'

Not a little reluctantly, Daniel put his index finger against the hollow. There was no bone there.

'You push, Daniel. Just a mite. Not too hard.'

Daniel did as he was told. The skin was elastic and dipped in.

'Jus' consider,' No-Head said, 'that little spongy feelin' is my brain.'

The following day, they drove the steers along the corridor cut through the chaparral. One tried to break into the cover but Daniel turned it. Where the cut passage ended, No-Head kept lookout. If anyone wanted to attack them it would be here, where the herd was vulnerable, stretched out in a long line and sparsely guarded.

Once out of the chaparral, the steers were gathered into a small herd and driven north-east across a plain of tall grass interrupted only occasionally by a tree or small area of cover. Whoever rode at the head of the herd kept an eye out.

'Fine lan'!' No-Head remarked. 'If I was of a mind t' settle me down, reckon it'd be here, with all this *galleta*.'

'What is *galleta*?' Daniel enquired.

'*Galleta*'s this here grass,' No-Head answered. 'Real dandy for steers. They'll put on a poun' o' weight a day eatin' this.'

Daniel frequently accompanied the person riding point, checking their direction with the compass, marking off their progress on Matt's map with a small indelible pencil. Although he had no sextant, Daniel also kept a sharp eye on the sun, working out its angle with a straight stick stuck in a gopher hole and computing it with No-Head's silver pocket watch. In a landscape with very few landmarks it was no easy matter maintaining an accurate heading. At night, by taking a bearing on the Pole Star, Daniel attempted to assure himself that his daytime readings had been accurate. He believed that he was maintaining the correct direction to within a degree or so.

When they camped that night, it was under the only tree visible for over a mile in any direction. Jesus drove the camp wagon right up to the trunk, Trinity's little tent being erected alongside it. As they settled down to sleep, the moon rose over the horizon.

Daniel could not take his eyes off it. It seemed huge, filling half the sky, tinted orange; he could plainly make out every crater on its surface.

'Ain't that somethin'?' No-Head remarked. 'Makes you feel real small, don't it?'

In the distance, a coyote started calling. It was a mournful howl interrupted by an occasional short yap.

''s long as he's callin', we ain't got no worry,' No-Head commented. 'He ain't one to sing when there's danger 'bout. An' danger for him is men, be they red, white or blue. You know what they call that?' he went on, jutting his chin at the horizon.

Daniel shook his head.

'That there's a coyote moon, that is. In native talk, coyote an' the moon go back a long way.'

When Daniel was woken to take his turn riding circle and watching over the steers, the moon was high and full, the stars quenched by its presence. The land was bathed in a cold, flat light that allowed the world no colour. The coyote still howled intermittently, responding to others calling on a low ridge in the very far distance.

Comforted by the coyotes' conversation, Daniel felt at ease as he rode circle. The steers were well settled, many of them sitting in the long grass, chewing the cud. Their breath smelled sweet on the still air. In places, only their long horns were to be seen above the grass heads.

Satan walked very slowly, almost plodding round the steers that had instinctively grouped themselves together for protection from predators long since extinct. It was all Daniel could do to stay awake.

Chapter 6

★

THE QUICK AND THE DEAD

The morning was uncharacteristically overcast, the air oppressive and humid. The steers were restless and frequently broke away; Daniel and Trinity kept busy bringing them back into the herd.

When they halted at noon, it was at a spring leading into a narrow creek lined by live oaks, their long branches convoluted and gnarled as if they were arthritic. In an attempt to try and find even the lightest of breezes, Daniel climbed into one of the trees and settled himself into a fork about twenty feet above ground. From there, he could see several hundred yards down the tunnel to where the trees formed over the creek.

He had been there for about ten minutes when a movement about fifty yards down the bank of the creek caught his eye. At first, he thought it was a deer coming down to drink but, as he watched, it materialized into a man, moving slowly at a crouch. He was wearing a buckskin jacket with fringed sleeves over a dirty cotton shirt, and a battered, wide-brimmed felt hat.

Daniel dropped to the ground. The others were nowhere to be seen. Even Jesus was absent, a hundred yards away at the spring collecting clean water in a wooden pail. Daniel slid under the camp wagon and, slowly pulling his Navy Colt from its holster, cocked it. Stooping behind a fallen tree trunk, the man surveyed the camp. Daniel kept still. After a minute, the intruder retreated. As soon as he was gone, Daniel ran to the tree trunk. If the man's trail consisted of bare feet or smooth moccasin leather, he knew he was an Indian. Yet the dusty soil bore the perfect imprint of a hob-nailed boot.

As soon as the others returned, Daniel reported the event to them and showed them the intruder's footprints.

'Good you made no move,' No-Head remarked. 'Had you done so, he'd've skinned you alive. He ain't no ordinary thief, nor's he a cattle rus'ler as you an' me might know 'em. No, sir! This is a real dang'rous piece o' work. We'd best keep a double watch from here t' th' Red River.'

Late that afternoon, they arrived at a small and shallow rain-fed lake, the banks devoid of vegetation and pitted with the footprints of the multitude of animals that drank there. No-Head pointed out the spoor of not only steers and shod horses but also deer, javelinas, mustangs, bobcats and a mountain lion. None were fresh. On the far bank lay the skeletons of half a dozen cattle, well picked over by buzzards, several of which perched expectantly on the bones.

'We'll press on,' No-Head decided. 'Ain't nothing here but mud an' putrefaction. We got 'nough water, Jesus?'

'*Si, señor*,' the Mexican replied. 'We got water for three days.'

'Right!' said No-Head. He stood up in his stirrups before easing himself back down into his saddle. 'Move 'em out.'

Daniel was about to turn the lead steer when, at the far end of the lake, there appeared three men on horseback. Behind them was a train of seven fully laden *burros*. One of the men raised his arm and called out a greeting. Daniel saw he was wearing a white cotton shirt and that the sleeves of his buckskin jacket were fringed.

He rode to No-Head's side at a steady trot, trying not to seem alarmed.

'That's the man who—' he began.

'I figured one of 'em was,' No-Head replied. 'They been trailin' us for an hour or two.'

'What do we do?' Daniel asked.

'Keep on our toes. We's got us some trouble.'

'Will they steal our steers?'

'No!' No-Head replied. 'They's out to kill 'em. Us, too. Them steers 'cross th' lake didn't die o' thirst. They was shot. You see anythin' odd about them carcasses?'

Daniel peered through the bright sunlight at them. They seemed to be just skeletons with a few shreds of dried meat hanging off them.

'No,' he said.

'Look again,' No-Head answered. 'They ain't got no skin. Buzzards don' gen'rally eat th' skin. Leastways, not lest they's real hungry and they done ate all th' meat. Them' – he cast a quick glance at the three men who were slowly making their way round the lake towards them – 'them's hide-rustlers. That's what them *burros* is carryin'. Hides.' He took a fleeting look across the lake. 'Reckon this might be one of their fav'rite ambushin' places. Bet if we was to look in the brush here abouts, we'd find us some skel'tons of the two-legged vari'ty . . .'

'How do, pilgrim?' one of the men greeted them affably. 'Where y'all headin'?'

'North a'ways,' No-Head replied noncommittally.

'Th' name's Stamp. Where y'all from?' enquired the buckskin-clad rustler.

'South. San Antone way.'

'An' you's doin' this with two Mexxie *vaqueros*, a boy and girl?'

'We're up t' th' task,' No-Head replied.

'You got some fine beeves there,' Stamp remarked, changing the subject and nodding in the direction of the herd. 'Got some good flesh on 'em.'

'We ain't drivin' 'em hard,' No-Head replied, not taking his eyes off Stamp.

'No sense,' answered Stamp. 'Just wear 'em down t' hoof 'n' horn.'

As they spoke, one of the men dismounted and started along the line of *burros*, ostensibly checking on their loads. Daniel watched him. At the fifth *burro*, he ducked out of sight. Daniel slipped from his saddle.

'Ain't wise, son,' Stamp said, his hand moving to the buckle of his belt.

No-Head's Navy Colt was out of its holster in not much more than a second. To one side, Beto had one of the Spencer rifles cocked and levelled at the second man's belly.

'While your hand's there, you slip that buckle,' No-Head ordered. 'Fact, why don't you both do that?'

Stamp and the other man did as they were told, their gun belts falling to the earth.

'We don't mean you no harm,' the second man said with an ingratiating grin.

''s may be,' No-Head replied, 'but I sat at 'nough poker tables to reckon I know a bad hand when I seed one. Now,' he went on calmly, 'keep your hands where I can see 'em. One squeak out of you two little bush rats an' you done nibbled your last cob o' corn.'

Daniel ran doubled up towards the steers, which were still bunched together by the edge of the muddy lake. Crouching down, he looked through the forest of legs, edging forwards until he saw a human pair in amongst them. The cattle ignored him, moving slowly aside to let him through. Finally, he stood up, only just able to see over the steers' backs.

A man in a black Stetson was standing in the middle of the herd. He had his pistol out and was aiming it at one of the animals' heads.

Daniel lifted his Navy Colt clear of its holster. It seemed heavier than ever. His hand shook

116

slightly and his blood raced. He gently cocked it, hoping the metallic click of the hammer would go unheard and pointed the barrel at the rustler.

'Drop your gun,' he said loudly, hoping his voice sounded firm and authoritative.

The rustler did not obey but half-turned towards Daniel.

'Well, lookee here!' he exclaimed. 'If they ain't sent th' potboy t' do his papa's job. What you thinkin' of doin', runt? You pull a gun you'd best be of a mind t' use it.'

'I'll use it,' Daniel replied, aware his voice was faltering.

'I think me not,' the rustler answered. 'You ain't got th' stomach t' kill a man. It ain't like choppin' th' head off a chicken.'

With that, he swung round, his Navy Colt aimed directly at Daniel's head. Daniel could see right down the dark tunnel of the barrel. The man was not fifteen feet away.

'You ready, boy?' He smirked, showing a gap in his top front teeth. 'You be sure t' sen' me a telegraph. I sure would like to know what Heaven's like . . .'

Daniel tightened his finger on the trigger. The end of the barrel of the Colt quivered. His finger took up the trigger slack. The rustler's pistol fired. Daniel was suddenly knocked sideways by a solid punch between his shoulder blades. He stumbled yet still pulled his trigger. The recoil jarred his arm. The steers, galvanized into action, bucked away. Lying on the ground was the rustler. His pistol lay in the dirt out of his reach. A dark stain was rapidly seeping into his jacket. He scrabbled with one hand to staunch the flow of blood seeping from his shoulder. From beyond the steers, two more shots rang out in quick succession.

Daniel struggled to his feet. The air was grey-blue with acrid black powder smoke which made Daniel's nostrils itch. Behind him stood a longhorn steer. It tossed its head, the five-foot spread of its horns slicing through the air.

'Well, I heard of bein' saved by th' bell, but I ain't never heard of bein' saved by th' bull before.'

Daniel turned round. Behind him was No-Head, mounted on his horse.

'Y'all right, Daniel?'

'I think so,' Daniel replied. 'What happened?'

'This ol' bull got bit by a fly and he shook his head an' his long horn swung roun' an' sent you flyin'.'

No-Head dismounted.

'What about the other two?' Daniel enquired.

'Waitin' for th' buzzards,' No-Head replied enigmatically. 'So all's we got t' worry our heads 'bout is this little pile o' offal.'

He walked over to the rustler, who was now sitting up, blood running down his left arm. Daniel had hit him in the shoulder. Through a tattered hole in the man's jacket, he could see a ragged wound of raw flesh, splintered bone and red blood.

'You know what they do t' rus'lers in Texas?' No-Head went on to ask in a quiet voice. 'Hang 'em,' he continued, not waiting for an answer, 'which gives you a choice.' He stepped forwards and studied the rustler's wound.

'Your goddam brat done wing me,' the rustler grunted.

'He ain't no brat,' No-Head replied almost pensively. 'And he ain't mine. He's his own man.'

Beto rode up, followed by Trinity. They sat on their horses, watching.

No-Head walked a few paces from the rustler. 'Well, reckon I was wrong. You ain't got no choice,' he said softly. 'Your shoulder's busted pretty good, you're bleedin' like a stuck pig an' there ain't no trees 'roun' here t' hang you from.' He looked over his shoulder. 'Trinity, can you go fetch Jesus?'

Trinity turned her horse and trotted off. No-Head levelled his Colt at the rustler's head.

'If you's real quick, you useless sack o' dung, you can catch your frien's up at th' gates o' Hell.'

And he pulled the trigger.

Daniel sat with his knees hunched to his chin, hugging his shins and looking at flames dancing in the fire. Bats, living in a hole in the tree above his head, swung to and fro over the creek, picking off gnats and mosquitoes. He mulled over the events of the day in his mind.

After No-Head had killed the rustler, he and Jesus had tied a rope around his feet and dragged his body to the other side of the lake, where it was

propped up against a cattle carcass. The other two
rustlers were similarly dragged over and placed
beside him. No-Head wrote a notice on a sheet of
board from the camp wagon and hung it on one
of the bodies. It read:

Hide Russlers. Got What was comin to Em.

This done, No-Head cut the bales of hides off
the *burros* and set them free. They wandered off
into the brush, one of them braying loudly as if
laughing at its sudden freedom. The rustlers'
horses, each bearing a different brand, were un-
bridled and their saddles removed. Then they, too,
were given their liberty, No-Head whipping their
rumps to make them canter off. Trinity had asked
why they did not keep them but No-Head said they
would be too much trouble; someone, he
commented, might think they had stolen them.
From the rustlers' saddlebags, Beto removed six
boxes of bullets and sixty-five silver dollars. In
addition, he collected up their weapons, three rifles
and four pistols.

Daniel had eaten little of his meal, spending most of the time pushing cubes of dark meat around his plate, occasionally chewing on a few beans.

No-Head came and sat down beside him.

'You mus' eat somethin'. Need your strength. Drivin' steers ain't a job for weaklin's.'

Daniel edged some beans onto his fork.

'You musin' on the day?' No-Head asked.

Daniel nodded.

'Don't you give it no thought,' No-Head said. 'I recall it's tough that first time you shoot a man but if you hadn't done it you'd not be sittin' here now. He would be, like as not, wearing your hat, eatin' your beans and ridin' your horse.'

'Did you have to kill the others?' Daniel replied.

'Stamp was a sly binder,' No-Head answered. 'He went for a dainty little lady's piece tucked in his boot. It was him or me. As for th' other feller, he went for his rifle. Beto did what he was obliged to do by th' circ'mstance.'

From the direction of the creek came the sound of bull frogs. Suddenly, there was a loud *plop!* and the frogs fell instantly silent.

'Turtle,' No-Head said. 'He done eat one ol' bull frog so th' others stop their carousin'. Those fellers had good rifles, too. One's a Big Fifty . . .'

'What's a Big Fifty?' Daniel asked.

'That's a .50 Sharp,' No-Head answered. 'You can drop a bison with one o' them at a hundred yards.' He reached into his pocket and removed a tiny, four-barrelled pistol which almost entirely fitted in his hand. A filigree pattern upon the barrel was etched in gold. 'You ever seed one o' these? They call this a pepperbox.'

He pulled the trigger several times, the barrels revolving with an audible click. Daniel took it. The gun weighed a few ounces at most and nothing compared to his Navy Colt.

'Close up,' No-Head said, 'under ten feet or so, that's as deadly as it is dandy. Some pretty lady must've died a nasty death so Stamp could have this little bauble.'

'What are you going to do with it?' Daniel enquired.

'Gift it to Miss Trinity. One day, this might jus' come in handy for her.' He took Daniel's dish. 'You done with this chow?'

Daniel nodded again. No-Head picked up the fork and hungrily ate what was left.

'Un'erstan' this, Daniel,' he said, putting the dish on the ground and wiping his mouth with a piece of bread then eating it, crumbs adhering to the stubble on his chin, 'This ain't the reg'lar world we're in now. Ain't no lawmen or priests or judges or juries of twelve folk an' true. Where we is an' where we's goin' is beyond law an' order. Out here, you's th' judge, th' jury an' th' executioner, too. This is th' lan' of th' quick and the dead. And I assure you' – he put his hand on Daniel's shoulder – 'I ain't intendin' t' be one o' th' latter.' He looked up at the stars glinting through the branches overhead. 'We foun' us a real nice spot here,' he remarked. 'Soft grass, big tree, sweet water runnin' by. We should remember this for th' journey back.'

With that, No-Head picked up the dish, rose to his feet, swatted an insect biting his neck and walked over to the fire. Daniel watched him go. He liked No-Head and trusted him but he had, that day, seen the cold-blooded killer in him.

A few minutes later, No-Head returned on his

way to his horse: it was his turn to ride circle first that night.

'I know what's on your mind,' he said as he approached Daniel. 'You're thinkin' we should've fixed 'im, put a bandage on 'im, let 'im ride th' camp wagon. Get 'im to a doctor. Ain't that so?'

'Yes,' Daniel admitted.

'No point,' No-Head answered. 'Your bullet really mussed his shoulder. He was sure t' die inside th' hour. But, s'ppose we'd fixed 'im. Got a doctor who saw 'im through. What next? They'd only hang 'im. Reckon even he'd prefer a bullet to bouncin' on the end of a rope. An' there's no sayin' he wouldn't've shot us from his sick bed. Men like him have no honour and live by no rules. They got the mentality of snakes.'

With that, No-Head mounted his horse, turned its head and trotted off into the night, only the sound of his spurs telling Daniel where he was in the darkness.

As Daniel lay on his side next to the fire, his blanket pulled up to his chin, Beto snoring gently to one side and Jesus turning restlessly under the

125

wagon, he heard No-Head singing to settle the steers, quietening the dogies. It seemed bizarre to him that a grown man who had been scalped and left for dead, who had – not twelve hours before – shot two men, one in the head, should now be singing a mournful lullaby to calm a herd of cattle.

Chapter 7

★

CALLS-HIS-HORSE

Six days after the encounter with the hide-rustlers, they reached Mound City on the banks of the Red River. Daniel had expected at least a small cluster of houses, perhaps even a church, but all that existed was a low log cabin with a shingle roof and a small, empty corral. London, he thought, was a city; this place was not even a hamlet.

Leaving the cattle in Beto's charge on the side of a nearby hill, Daniel, Trinity and No-Head rode down to the building. Just as they reached it, a man appeared with a double-barrelled shotgun held across his chest. He wore a red flannel shirt and grey denim trousers with patches of buckskin sewn on at the knees. The legs of his trousers were tucked into high leather boots.

'Y'all tradin' or passin' by?' he demanded. 'If you's passin', keep movin'.'

'We's tradin',' No-Head replied. 'On our way north with fifty head.' He jerked his thumb in the direction of the herd.

At that moment, Daniel saw that the hammers on the shotgun were pulled back: the weapon was cocked.

'These yours?' the man asked, looking disparagingly at Daniel and Trinity.

'They're with me,' No-Head replied. 'Good kids, but they ain't kin.'

'Y'all empty your pieces. Now.' The man waved the muzzle of the shotgun to and fro, covering each of them by turn. 'I wan' t' see you do that.'

They all unloaded their weapons, putting the shells in their pockets and replacing the guns in their holsters.

The man uncocked the shotgun and said, 'Been robbed twice in ten months ... Name's Bryarly. R. T. Bryarly.'

They dismounted, tethered their horses to a rail and followed Mr Bryarly into the building.

The walls were lined with shelves but there was very little merchandise upon them. What he seemed to have most of were tins of beans, coffee and corned beef. At the far end of the room was a curtained-off area containing a bed and a seaman's chest with a heavy padlock on it.

Mr Bryarly leaned the shotgun against a sack of apples and poured out four mugs of coffee.

'Y' ain't got much on offer here,' No-Head observed.

'Stores come up th' river. River trade's my lifeline. Built me a jetty, but what with th' water droppin' on account of there bein' so little rain of late, an' with th' war an' all on, business ain't so brisk. Ain't seed a riverboat in two weeks.' Mr Bryarly slurped his coffee and asked, 'So what d' y'all want?'

No-Head purchased ten tins of corned beef, a pound of green coffee and a small stone jug of rum.

It was not that they needed these items. His reason for stopping here had been to glean news. By the time they had finished their coffee, they knew that the Indians were restless amongst themselves, stirred up – as Matt had predicted might be the case – by the enforced arrival of the Wacoes and Caddoes; there were no Blue Bellies for miles and to watch out for three hide-rustlers.

'No fear of them,' No-Head told Bryarly bluntly. 'Their own hides is now tannin' in the fires of Hell.'

Bryarly smiled wryly to himself at this news and remarked, 'Tried t' take me, they did. Hope Ol' Nick's stoked his fires up good for 'em.'

That evening, they brought the cattle in close to a pen by Bryarly's place and put the horses in the corral. As for Daniel and the others, when one of them was riding circle, the others slept around the stove on the earth floor of the cabin while Bryarly snored and grunted and farted on his bed behind the curtain.

At dawn, No-Head reconnoitred the river a mile in each direction from Bryarly's jetty. When he

returned he had decided where they would attempt
a crossing.

''bout half a mile downstream, it gets real
narrow,' he reported. 'Sandbar this side, sandbank
on th' opposite. Th' bank this side drops maybe ten
foot, but it ain't nothin' th' steers can't handle.'

As they saddled up, Bryarly came out of his
trading post.

'If y'all have a mind to,' he said, 'tell th' other
drovers you meet that there's a cup o' coffee here
and a good crossin' point.'

'Surely will,' No-Head assured him as they shook
hands. 'You take care now.'

They drove the cattle out of the pen and down
towards the river. As they passed Bryarly's place, the
man came out and waved to them.

At the riverbank, Daniel leaned back in the
saddle, stood back in the stirrups and rode Satan
down the drop. Straightening up, he edged the horse
across the sandbar, wending his way between the
rocks and trees carried down in a flood and strewn
over the sand. Pausing, he urged the horse into the
water, which barely came up to its belly. Behind

him, No-Head, Trinity and Beto drove the steers forward. They were reluctant to descend to the sandbar but, once the lead steer had scrabbled down the bank and into the river, the others followed, splashing across to the sandy beach on the far side, where Daniel herded them together. Last to cross the river was the camp wagon. Jesus had to struggle with the brake to stop the vehicle falling forwards down the drop and onto the dray horses but, after some minutes and throwing sand into the brake blocks to get the leather shoes to grip, he got the wagon into the river and cracked a short whip over the horses' rumps. They neighed and lunged forward. Roja, standing on the back board, lost his footing and fell into the river. When he reached the far bank he was dripping wet and had a humiliated look on his face.

'That's learned you a lesson, dog,' No-Head said.

Roja shook himself, lifted his lip in a smile snarl, lowered his head and feebly wagged his tail, water spraying out from the feathering.

'All right!' No-Head went on. 'I'll take pity on you, mutt! Most wouldn't. Up you come!'

Roja ran forward, leapt into the air and landed on No-Head's mount, just behind the saddle, where he stood balancing and moving to the motion of the walking horse.

'Move 'em out!' No-Head called and they started the cattle walking away from the river and into scattered brush and tall grassland.

For three days, as they made their way up through the foothills of the Ouachita Mountains, they were shadowed by a band of six Indians. No-Head spied them first. They were on foot, accompanied by a dog, and made no effort to hide themselves. During the daylight, they kept up with the herd, sometimes jogging along parallel to it, sometimes ranging ahead. At night, they camped half a mile away, their fire plainly visible.

'They must o' seed th' smoke of our fire or th' dust from th' steers right from the time we crossed th' river,' No-Head decided. 'That mus' be what brung 'em in.'

The following day, the Indians approached to within a hundred yards but still kept their distance.

Even when No-Head waved to them, they did not acknowledge his greeting.

'What tribe're they?' Trinity asked.

No-Head turned in his saddle and squinted at a ridge along which the Indians were moving in a line, the dog taking up the rear at a steady lope.

'Can't make 'em out too clear. Reckon they's Choctaws. They's shaved their heads down the sides but lef' a block o' hair standin' down the middle,' No-Head decided at length. 'That's Choctaw style, best as I knowed it. B'sides, they don't mean us no harm anyways. If they was out for blood or steers, we'd see neither hide nor hair of 'em till they was on us, a-whoopin' an' a-slashin' with those tomahawk axes o' theirs.'

When the herd stopped for the night, Daniel and Trinity drove the cattle into a small dead-end *arroyo* for safekeeping. Daniel took first turn to ride circle although this really only required sitting on Satan and not letting steers out of the *arroyo*. Yet they were in no mood to move. Coyotes yelped close by and the cooler air of the mountains seemed to have settled the herd. They mostly lay down on the ground and chewed the cud in the darkness.

'What if the Indians appear in the night?' Daniel asked No-Head.

'No fear of that,' he replied. 'They seldom move themselves about in th' darkness for fear o' spirits an' suchlike.'

Daniel sat in the saddle and fought to stay awake. It was not long before the moon rose, bright enough to cast shadows. At midnight, Beto relieved him and he slid under his blanket to fall straight into a dreamless slumber.

When Daniel woke at dawn it was to find a roaring fire going, with waffles cooking on a griddle and the smoke-blackened coffee pot simmering on the edge of the embers. Jesus was turning the waffles and Trinity was brushing through her hair. Across the fire from them squatted five Indians. They all wore buckskin trousers with multi-coloured woollen blankets draped round their shoulders. Two sported eagle feathers in their hair and all had decorated leather headbands. On their feet they wore moccasins with leather leggings. Two possessed flintlock muskets, the others bows and quivers of arrows with stone points.

'Got us some guests to break our fast with,' No-Head observed, pouring himself a coffee and adding a drop of condensed milk to it.

Daniel shook his head to waken himself.

'Where's the sixth one?' he wondered aloud.

'Now that's like a kind o' mystery,' Trinity replied.

'The Choctaw's one o' them tribes they call civilized, so I don't reckon we's in risk of a haircut,' No-Head Nolan said. 'On t'other hand, I ain't never met an Indian you could afford to take your eyes off. Wherever that brave be, you can be sure he's up to no good as far as we's concerned.'

Daniel leaned forward, took one of the waffles off the griddle, broke it in half and dipped it in a jar of molasses, the syrup dripping onto the ground between his feet. As he took his first bite, he caught, out of the corner of his eye, a movement under the tree where the horses were tethered. The sixth Indian was kneeling there, untying Satan's reins. He then lay them across the horse's neck and, in one move, swung himself up onto the horse's bare back.

Satan seemed to quiver. The Indian, crouching down, edged the horse forward.

Suddenly, he jammed his heels into the horse's side, Satan going from a stand to a canter in less than ten feet.

Dropping the waffle, and spitting out what there was of it in his mouth, Daniel tried to whistle twice in quick succession. He couldn't. The molasses were sticking up his teeth. Grabbing No-Head's mug of coffee, he took a gulp, swilled it around his mouth and spat it out. Pursing his lips, he whistled Satan's signal and shouted, 'Stop!'

Satan instantly stuck his two front feet forwards and came to an abrupt halt. The Indian on his back was thrown forward onto his neck and fell to the ground. Daniel whistled again and called out, 'Come by!'

The horse gingerly stepped over the Indian, who was sitting on the ground rubbing his leg, and turned to trot in Daniel's direction. As his hindquarters passed over the Indian his tail went up and the inevitable roll of dung fell free to hit the Indian squarely on the head.

For a moment, the Indians by the fire watched in amazement before rolling on the ground in paroxysms of laughter, calling out to their friend and pointing at him.

'What are they saying?' Daniel asked.

'Well,' said No-Head, 'I ain't too good at Choctaw speak but I don't reckon it's too p'lite.'

Satan came and stood beside Daniel, his head down and the reins hanging free. The would-be thief walked sheepishly over to join his companions, who slapped him on the back and wiped their hands on his buckskin trousers. The tallest of the Indians looked at Daniel and spoke to him. At the same time, he moved his hands in Daniel's direction, as if he were swimming in mid-air.

'What's he saying?' Daniel asked, afraid he was having a spell cast on him.

'He's givin' you an Indian name,' No-Head explained. 'See, all Indians have names 'bout somethin' in their lives. Baby's born when there's a part eclipse of the moon so they call him "Half-Moon", or there's a wolf bayin' so they call him "Howlin'

Wolf". That movin' with his hands is his wipin' away your past name and givin' you a new one. Later in their lives, they get a new name, like when they's made a brave or become men. Now you're gettin' one.'

'Do you know what it is?' Daniel enquired. If he was to be renamed, he considered, he ought to know as what.

'Reckon I do,' No-Head replied, grinning. 'They's namin' you "Calls-His-Horse".'

'Reckon they'll rename th' other guy "Poopin' Horse"?' Trinity suggested.

They broke camp and moved the herd out of the *arroyo*, turning the steers northwards once more. The six Indians raised their hands in a farewell salute, jogging off southwards.

'Why do they call them civilized tribes?' Daniel asked as he rode point alongside No-Head.

'See, it's like this,' No-Head replied. 'Some o' they tribes done took to th' white man's ways. Those Choctaws was wearin' pants like you an' me. Most Indians don't do that. They'll wear breechcloths like little aprons made o' leather t' protect their privates. But th' Pawnees, th' Chickasaws, th' Cherokees, th' Choctaws an' a mess o' others's different. Fact is, I've even heard tell th' Cherokees an' th' Seminoles's siding with us 'gainst th' Blue Bellies.'

For the next three days, they rode on through the mountains, the steers kicking up less dust than on the plains but occasionally stumbling over the stony terrain. Twice, Daniel spied bears lingering in the trees but they did not approach the herd, preferring to slink off deeper into the woodland. Jesus worked hard to control the camp wagon, threading it carefully through the smaller gaps in the undergrowth. For the steeper descents, he and No-Head would tie a fallen tree to the back of the wagon with a rope, the log dragging behind, acting as an anchor might in a storm-tossed sea. Gradually, the landscape flattened as they descended once more to the plains, the rocky slopes being replaced by grass and brush prairie.

At noon on the fourth day, storm clouds began to gather to the east. No-Head called a halt.

'Bunch th' steers up,' he commanded. 'We's in for a blow. Las' thing we want is 'em splitting up.'

The sky darkened. Far off to the east appeared jags of lightning followed by long, low rumbles of thunder that rolled across the featureless landscape. No-Head dismounted and removed his slicker from his saddle roll. A large oilskin coat, it covered not just himself but his saddle, pack and a good bit of his horse as well. Daniel and the others followed suit. On the camp wagon, Jesus pulled the tarpaulin over and hunched himself up on the seat.

When the rain came, it was sudden and heavy. One moment, the air was clear, the next the rain pelted down, the drops huge and hard, kicking up craters of dust on the ground, drumming on Daniel's hat and running in rivulets down the folds in his slicker. When he held his hand out, his cupped palm collected enough water for him to drink in a mere matter of seconds. The steers plodded on. One or two broke rank when lightning struck a dead mesquite some way to the rear, igniting it.

'Dismount!' No-Head yelled.

Daniel obeyed, puzzled as to why, at a time when

141

the steers might take to their heels, they should be getting off their horses.

'Think on it,' No-Head said, realizing Daniel's bemused look. 'That ol' tree' – he pointed at the mesquite that was now smouldering – 'ain't much higher than you or me. An' lightning strikes things that're higher than most. Now speakin' pers'nally, I don't fancy th' idea o' bein' fried like a prairie oyster. Don't reckon my horse do, neither.'

They walked on, leading their horses by their reins into a shallow depression, dismounting and making the horses lie down. Jesus steered the camp wagon after them. After a while, the storm ceased, the lighting retreating to strike the hills to the south. Soon, the storm was little more than a memory, the sun hot again, a thin steam rising off the hot ground and the rumps of the horses. Only Roja looked bedraggled: that was not just because he had got wet but because he had taken to rolling in damp buffalo chips in the bottom of the depression.

Late in the afternoon, they came to the dried-up bed of a wide river along the banks of which grew a number of pecan and mesquite trees. Beto paused, dismounted and stood in the centre of the riverbed, kneeling down and pressing his ear to a large flat stone. He remained immobile for several minutes before he stood up.

'What d' you reckon, Beto?' No-Head asked.

Beto remounted his horse and answered, 'Is no way to be sure, *señor*.'

No-Head dismounted from his horse, kneeling and pressing his ear to the ground. For a long moment, the only sounds to be heard were the sawing of crickets and the snuffling of the horses.

'I think we'll wait awhile,' he decided, getting to his feet.

'Wait for what?' Daniel asked.

'Well, Daniel,' No-Head said, 'you look back south.'

Behind him, way out on the horizon, Daniel saw two dark thunder heads rising high into the sky, flattening out at the top. Beneath them, the sky was a dense grey.

'They's still making heavy rain,' Beto explained, 'An' that rain's got to go somewhere, *señorito*.'

'So we jus' bide a little while,' No-Head carried on, 't' make sure it ain't comin' our way.'

They turned the steers into a wide area of tall grass, Beto riding circle.

Daniel and Trinity sat on their horses on the banks of the dried-up riverbed. The air was warm and still and, from under the shade of the pecan trees, all was peaceful. Daniel rested his hands on his saddlehorn and allowed himself to doze.

Gradually, he became aware of a cool breeze blowing over him. It seemed to move under the trees rather than through them. Satan began to pad the ground with his front hooves. Then, quite suddenly, Daniel heard a roaring sound. It seemed to be coming nearer and nearer, accelerating by the second. Satan started to back step, turn and edge away from the riverbed. Trinity's horse followed suit.

Suddenly, a wall of water five feet high, churning over and over, muddy and filled with tree branches, rocks and snakes, came rolling down the riverbed. Of their own volition the two horses turned and galloped up the side of a low ridge nearby, upon the crest of which were No-Head and Beto, holding the herd back.

As the water rolled by, those snakes which had not been injured in the tumult slithered free onto the bank, heading for high ground. One of the reptiles, a huge diamondback rattlesnake, slithered quickly towards Trinity's horse. It shied away from the reptile, then reared up. She clung to the saddle, but to no avail. Her horse wanted to be rid of her, to lose the weight on its back. She fell to the ground, winded. The rattler disappeared but its place was taken by a long, thin, black snake. It reared back as if to strike the air. As it opened its mouth to bare its fangs, Daniel saw that the inside of its mouth was white.

Pulling his Navy Colt from its holster, he knew he was not a good enough shot to hit the snake but thought that if he could hit the ground near its head he might divert it. The risk was that a ricochet might hit Trinity. Yet there was nothing for it. She was scrabbling with her hands in the dust, trying to get up, and her frantic movements were drawing the snake's attention.

Better a bullet than a bite, Daniel thought and he fired.

The snake was not deflected from its purpose. He fired again. Gravel spattered over the snake's head but this seemed only to infuriate it.

'Keep still!' Daniel shouted to Trinity.

No-Head rode up. 'Still your hand!' he exclaimed. 'That cottonmouth thinks your fingers's a frog, a bird or a mouse or somesuch.'

Jesus ran over from the wagon carrying a shotgun across his chest. Without stopping, he threw it horizontally to No-Head, who caught and cocked it in one action.

'Daniel,' he yelled, 'move aside a ways an' th' minute I fire, you dash right in an' let Trinity get on t' Satan.'

Daniel urged Satan forwards towards Trinity. No-Head raised the shotgun to his shoulder, took aim and fired. The snake was instantly cut in half, each section writhing and thrashing, its head striking in mid-air. Trinity scrabbled to her feet, took hold of Daniel's saddle and swung herself up onto Satan's rump. Satan trotted up the ridge.

'Close call,' said No-Head.

Daniel could feel Trinity shaking where she held onto him with her arms around his waist.

'If that mocc'sin had bit me, I wouldn't be seein' Dark Creek again,' she said pensively.

As she spoke, Daniel remembered Matt's words as they parted from him north of Austin: *I don't want t' find one of you was bit by a rattler, drowned in a flood nor struck by lightning nor nothin'.*

'Well,' he replied, 'we did say we would watch out for each other.'

Trinity smiled and replied, 'Well, I sure do owe you one.'

Chapter 8

★

TWO SHALLOW GRAVES

Daniel rode up to the crest of a low ridge and looked over it. A mile or so ahead was a river valley, the banks wide apart and the water dark green under the sunny sky. Between him and the riverbank he could make out a track. It consisted of little more than two wagon-wheel ruts with grass growing tall between them. Throughout the length he could see, it followed the line of the river. Not far off to his left was a square copse of trees contained within a derelict rail-and-post fence. Beneath the trees he could make out a number of wooden head-boards.

'Right spot on,' he said aloud, grinning to him-self with pleasure. Navigating across the prairie, he considered, was little different from navigating across the sea: for islands there were trees.

He rode back to the herd and reported what he had seen. No-Head congratulated him and Beto reached across and patted him on the shoulder.

'You're a clever boy, *señorito*,' he said. 'Is a long way and you have done it right to the place.'

Daniel turned Satan and rode down to the grave-yard, dismounting and wrapping the reins around one of the fence-rails. Entering the burial ground, he wandered amongst the tombs, looking at the inscriptions on the sun-bleached head boards: *Ewan McAllister – '49er*; *Art Menken*; *Willem Herben – Dutchman, California bound: never made it*. One grave marker consisted solely of a miner's broad spade with a broken haft.

Reading these words, Daniel considered how, but for the grace of God, he could have, and might yet, end up like these men who had been chasing a dream only to have it for ever move out of reach, like the end of a rainbow. There was, he thought, a pretty fair chance that he too might end up in a grave on the prairie with a wooden marker that, in fifty years, would have vanished, cracked by sun and snow and consumed by termites.

Mounting up again, Daniel turned Satan towards the river. A hundred yards or so along the track, he consulted the map Matt had given him and found a narrow path that wended its way towards the river through a band of thick scrub. Where the scrub thinned it started to descend steeply down to the river. No-Head, Beto and Trinity rode up.

'Now this ain't an easy matter,' No-Head remarked, looking down the slope. 'The steers'll find it heavy goin'. We's likely t' have t' let them go down in small parcels, otherwise they're like t' fall atop each other. With them horns, that'll mean some serious inj'ry. Only good thing in our favour is th' path runs down a gully. That'll keep them in a line.'

As they rode back to the herd, No-Head gave his orders.

'This is how we'll do it. Me, Beto an' Trinity's t' ride down firs' on t' th' sandy river shore. Daniel, you drive the steers down that gully, not more 'n five at a time. When they reach th' bottom, we'll keep 'em together. When th' last ones are through, y' come on down. When they's all by th' water, th' four of us'll drive 'em across t' th' island. From there, we'll take 'em on over th' narrow water t' th' far side. There, Trinity, you keep 'em bunched up. Daniel, Beto an' me'll go back an' give Jesus a hand down th' bank. Guess we better jus' get on wit' th' job. Th' secret here's to take it real slow 'n' easy.'

As the other three disappeared over the edge of the gully, Daniel turned Satan towards the herd and cut out five steers. These he drove at nothing more than a walk towards the entrance to the gully where, after a moment's hesitation, the first steer started down the slope. He did not need to drive them down it. The angle was such that they had no choice but to descend.

It was a slow process, but the remainder of the herd went down the slope without any difficulty. Finally Daniel followed the last one down to join the others on the sandbar below.

'Th' river's quite deep here,' No-Head observed, 'an' the current's fast. Th' rain done seed to that. So we'll have t' drive them in at th' upstream end of th' bar. That ways, they should reach th' island about halfway down. Luck'ly, th' water on t'other side of th' island don't seem t' be in such a hurry.'

The steers were driven up the sandbar and then into the water. No-Head went ahead of the herd, his horse swimming strongly with the lead steer following. Daniel, Trinity and Beto took up the rear. Just as No-Head had predicted, they landed halfway down the island.

'So far, so good!' No-Head exclaimed, as he turned the lead steer into the channel between the island and the far bank. Not only was it comparatively narrow but it was also no deeper than a few feet. The steers crossed in one body to dry land.

Leaving the steers with Trinity, Daniel, No-Head and Beto returned across the river, rode along the sandbar and up the gully. At the top was Jesus and the camp wagon.

'Now, we's got us a dilemma,' said No-Head. 'Jesus can get th' wagon down th' gully t' th' sand-bar, jus' by riding th' brake. But that river's runnin' an' there's no way them dray horses can hold that wagon 'gainst th' current.'

'I have an idea,' said Daniel. 'The horses don't have to pull the wagon over. We can let the river do it for us.'

No-Head, Beto and Jesus exchanged looks. Here was a real greenhorn, fresh to driving steers, about to offer to get them over a river in flood.

'You reckon?' No-Head said somewhat sceptically.

'I reckon,' Daniel answered confidently and he underlined his strategy.

No-Head scratched his stubbled chin. It had been five days since he had last attempted a shave.

'What have we to lose, *señor*?' Beto said to No-Head.

'Wagonful of supplies, *compadre*,' No-Head replied bluntly, but he agreed to give Daniel's plan a try.

Under Daniel's instruction, they each tied their

three *riatas* into a long rope which was coiled up on the sandbar. Daniel then took one end and rode out across the river with it. Satan was a strong swimmer and, although he drifted some way down on the current, he easily made the far bank. Once there, Daniel rode upstream to where the bole of a huge tree that had been washed down in a previous flood had been half buried in the shore of the island. He tied the rope to it and signalled across to No-Head, who tied the other end of the rope to the upstream side of the camp wagon. When all was ready, Jesus cracked the whip and the horses pulled the wagon into the river. The current quickly took hold of it and began to carry it away but the rope held tight and the tree stump, acting as a pivot, swung the wagon around and into the island, the horses pulling it up the bank.

'Now, that's what I call some kind o' thinkin'!' No-Head remarked as they all gathered on the island. 'I mus' say I thought it was a cockamamie idea at th' start but you done pull it off, boy!' He slapped Daniel on the back and lightly punched his arm.

Crossing the wagon over the narrower channel from the island to the far shore was easy and, in a matter of minutes, Jesus was driving the camp wagon onto dry land once more, Roja looking out over the back board, his tongue hanging out in a canine smile and his tail beating a tattoo on a barrel of flour.

Daniel dismounted and took a compass reading. In his mind he heard Matt's instruction: *Once over th' river, bear jus' east o' north.*

A mile in front, a ridge ran west to east along the horizon. No-Head signalled a halt.

'Beto, you 'n' Trinity keep th' herd here. Bunch 'em up. Daniel, you ride with me. Check your piece ain't empty.'

Daniel eased his Navy Colt out of its holster. Every chamber was loaded.

'We'll move on now,' No-Head said. 'Jus' you 'n' me. Ride on my left side. Don't go movin' ahead.'

'What's up?' Daniel asked, his voice quiet with apprehension.

'Sniff th' air,' No-Head replied.

Daniel could only smell the scents of the plants Satan's hooves crushed or brushed against and said so.

'Pull up.'

Daniel reined Satan in.

'Do it again. Good lungful.'

For a moment he still smelled nothing; then it came to him. It was a faint tang of wood smoke. Satan padded the ground with one of his front hooves.

'What is it?' Daniel enquired at not much more than a whisper.

'Put it this way,' No-Head replied. 'Fires don't light themselves.'

They walked the horses on, dismounting just below the top of the ridge. Edging forwards at a crouch, and using a dense patch of sage brush for cover, they peered over the ridge at the land beyond. Some way off stood a rectangular palisade of logs, in which were three of what looked to Daniel to be bunkhouses. Nearby was the smouldering wooden frame of a fourth building.

'That's a fort, I reckon,' No-Head declared. 'Leastways, it was.'

'What do you think's happened?' Daniel mused.

'No ways of tellin' lest we moseys on down there,' replied No-Head and, remounting, he tapped the side of his horse with his heels.

They approached the fort with caution, both of them keeping a sharp eye on the palisades. Yet the only thing they saw moving was a buzzard perching on the top of the main gate archway. It was preening itself and stropping its beak on a timber crossbeam.

'That don't bode well,' No-Head observed as the large bird took to the wing. 'But then again it do. Where them devil's chickens's roostin', there ain't no people. Not livin' ones anyways.'

The main gate had been wrenched free of its hinges and hung awry. They rode through. Here and there, blue Union Army uniforms were scattered about amongst a litter of empty food cans, ammunition boxes, bottles and personal effects.

Daniel and No-Head dismounted once again, Daniel picking up a square of paper that blew against the side of his boot, to be held there by the breeze. It was scorched and brittle along one edge. Upon it was some neat, cursive writing.

My darling Martha, he read, *I miss you and baby Jo-Jo mightily. It's real lonesome out here, just the yowlin coyotes and the humm of the wind. The Injiands seem to have moved off deeper into the territory. Theys strange-looking folk for sure, but peaceable enuff, I reckon . . .*

'What you got there?' No-Head asked.

'It's a letter from one of the soldiers.'

No-Head peered at it flapping in the breeze between Daniel's fingers.

'Do you know what it says? I ain't too fond o' readin' an' writin' an' suchlike.'

'Nothing really,' Daniel answered. Somehow, it seemed wrong to be reading another's private letter. He let the paper go. It danced on the breeze and blew into the smouldering building where, landing on a glowing spar, it briefly flared.

Surveying his surroundings, Daniel saw a pair of uniform gloves lying on the ground against the palisade.

'I wouldn't if I was you,' No-Head said as Daniel took a step towards them. 'That second glove ain't

crumpled. Y' know what that means?' Daniel
looked puzzled. 'It means th' hand's still in it.
That's what them buzzards's been peckin' at. Ain't
likely t' be a pretty sight.' He nudged the glove with
his boot. A swarm of flies escaped from within it to
settle on the palisade.

Behind one of the bunkhouses were four fresh
mounds of earth, laid out in a line.

'You think the Indians . . .' Daniel began
tentatively.

'No,' No-Head answered with certainty. 'You see
any arrows any place? An' Indians don't dig graves.
An' you lookee here.' He pointed into the nearest
bunkhouse, the door of which was wide open.
'Them shelves ain't got no cans o' food on 'em. Th'
Indians don't take cans o' chow. They don't know
how t' get int' them. No sir, this is th' work of our
boys.'

'Our boys?' Daniel queried.

'Th' army of th' Confederacy. They took all the
stores. You see any guns lyin' round?'

'But why have they burned a building?'

'So's th' Blue Bellies can't use it,' No-Head

explained. 'It's my guess they'd've burned the whole dang thing had they th' inclination or th' time. They must've been in a hurry. Now,' he went on, 'it's up t' us t' finish th' job. Go tell th' others to come on over.' Daniel rode off, returning to find No-Head collecting brushwood.

While Beto and Jesus went through the buildings, checking that there were no provisions remaining that they could use, and Trinity watered the steers and horses at a shallow pan a short distance away, Daniel and No-Head piled the brushwood against the palisade and buildings. Once everyone was clear, No-Head dowsed the brushwood with lamp oil and a barrel of pitch and set it alight. By the time they left, the palisade and the three remaining bunkhouses were burning fiercely.

Daniel rubbed his eyes. Staring all day long into the distance, he had discovered, was apt to play tricks on them after a few hours; but surely, he thought, not one of such magnitude as this. He blinked and looked again. It was definitely not a mirage. Half a mile or so ahead there seemed to be a small yacht with sun-bleached canvas sails moving across the landscape, heading west. Perhaps, he considered, they were coming up to the Arkansas River: and yet No-Head had said they were a couple of days from it and Daniel's own estimation agreed with him.

Approaching nearer, Daniel watched as the yacht transformed into a long wagon pulled by four oxen. The canvas awning was in tatters. No one appeared to be steering.

No-Head drew the herd up.

'Don't like it,' he declared. ''tain't right. Something smells about it.' He turned to Daniel, Trinity and Beto. 'Loosen your guns. I think we's in for trouble.'

Side by side, they rode slowly forward, not once taking their eyes off the wagon. As they drew near, the oxen stopped, turning their heads in their direction. One of them belled mournfully. Nearer still, Daniel could see into the wagon. The contents were strewn about, a barrel of seed corn split open, a chest of clothes fallen on its side and a box of books tumbling its contents into the seed corn. Leaning against the side of the wagon were a man and a woman. The side of the man's head was covered in congealed blood, which had seeped onto the shoulder of the woman's white cotton blouse. Her hair was tangled as if wind-swept. As her eyes alighted on Daniel, she fumbled for a rifle lying at her side and tried to lift it up but the barrel was wedged under the box of books.

Daniel dismounted, joined by Trinity. He ran to the wagon and swung himself up and over the side. Trinity, meanwhile, grabbed hold of the oxen's traces and pulled them tight, wrapping them round the driving seat so the beasts would not move off. Getting the rifle free, the woman attempted to aim it at Daniel.

'It's all right, ma'am,' he said. 'I mean you no harm.'

She lowered the rifle. Daniel reached forward and uncocked it. No-Head slid from his saddle and, climbing into the wagon, looked to the man, removing the woman's arms from around his shoulders and feeling on his neck for a pulse. Trinity lowered herself next to the woman.

'Is Ted all right?' the woman asked in a whisper.

'He's alive,' said No-Head, 'but we'll have t' tend him. He's lost a lot o' blood.'

Mingled with the spilt corn were spent cartridge cases.

'What happened here?' Daniel asked.

'We was chased,' the woman said. 'I managed to fire back. I know I shouldn't've. It's not the Lord's way, to take the life of another. But I guessed that I might put 'em off some. But then they hit Ted and when we slowed they caught us up an' robbed us.' She pointed to a small leather bag lying on the wagon boards. 'Three hundred and ninety dollars. We sold our store in Charleston an' joined a wagon train. We was heading west.'

'Trinity, go get Jesus,' ordered No-Head. 'Daniel, help me here.'

Together, Daniel and No-Head eased the unconscious man onto a sack of flour.

'What's happened to him?' Daniel asked.

No-Head looked at the man's neck and said, 'Been hit in th' collar bone. Bullet's deflected up an' creased his neck. Nicked his jugular, I'd guess. No tellin' what damage's been done under this mess o' dried blood.'

Jesus arrived with the camp wagon and No-Head set about cleaning up the wound with a mixture of water and vinegar.

'Trick I learned off that ol' trapper what saved me that time,' he said. 'Th' vin'gar cleans th' wound, makes it so's you don't get no infection in. Stings like billy-oh but I don't think this 'ere's likely t' make much complaint, d' you?'

The man's collar bone had been shattered. No-Head carefully removed the small splinters of bone from the wound, dropping them over the side of the wagon. Cleaning the neck injury caused the wound to start to weep again. No-Head tied a bandage around the man's throat. After a short while, the man regained consciousness.

Before he could speak, Trinity touched his brow and said, 'Don't fret none, now. We'll get t' some-place safe where they got a proper doctor.'

The woman held the man's hand. 'I'm still here, Ted,' she said in a quiet voice.

'Where's Joely?' he replied in a whisper.

'Joely's gone, Ted, Joely's gone.'

It was then Daniel noticed a child's smock lying in the corner of the wagon. A wave of sadness swept over him.

'What happened to Joely?' asked Trinity in a broken voice.

'We was driving hard,' the woman replied in little more than a murmur. 'They was gaining on us and Joely, well, she stood up and we hit this gopher hole and then she was gone.' A tremor ran through the woman as if she had suddenly been hit by a cold blast of air, a blue norther heading down from the Rockies.

Daniel glanced at No-Head. He was tight-lipped, his expression sombre. Understanding, Daniel dipped his head in respect. Hitting the ground hard would almost certainly have resulted in the child's death. If she had survived, the pursuers would have given no thought to murder.

'Who was doin' th' chasin', ma'am?' asked No-Head as he tied the last knot in the man's bandage.

'They weren't Indians, that's for sure, but neither was they Blue Bellies. There was 'bout twenty of them and they talked English. That's all I know.'

'How long since all this come t' pass?' No-Head wanted to know.

'Maybe four hours. I can't say. Sun was still climbin'.'

For a few minutes, No-Head was silent. 'I reckon,' he said finally, 'we got no choice. These scum ain't far away an' we don't want t' run int' 'em if we can avoid it. We need some safe place to rest up till they're gone from hereabouts. Best I guess we can do is head for Perryman's trading store. T' th' best of my recollection that's about a day an' a half's travellin' up this track to the west. I met Lewis Perryman one time when I was passin' through this territ'ry. He's a fair guy an' his trading post's a sturdy place.'

They transferred the man and woman to the camp wagon and offloaded as much of their supplies as they could. There was no way they could drive the homesteaders' oxen and wagon along with them, so Beto let the draught animals go and they abandoned the wagon by the side of the track after smashing the wheel spokes with an axe. Rounding up the herd that had drifted into the brush, they turned onto the track, continuing the route the homesteaders had been travelling.

That evening, they entered rolling country covered with light woodland. No-Head decided they would stop by a small pond at which they watered the cattle before bedding them down for the night. When Jesus had a fire going, Daniel climbed into the camp wagon with a mug of water for the man and a plate of beans for the woman. Neither of them moved. He put down the plate of food and felt for a pulse on their wrists. The man was dead, as was the woman.

Returning to the campfire, he lowered himself down next to Trinity, close to the flames. He felt puzzled and, despite his proximity to the fire, chilled.

'Why did she die?' he pondered aloud after a while. 'She was a little bruised but not really hurt.'

'I seed it b'fore,' said Trinity quietly. 'She'd jus' had enough. Weren't nothin' left f' her an' she wanted t' be with her loved ones.'

As the sun set, Jesus and Daniel dug two shallow

graves while Trinity collected stones to put upon them, to prevent the coyotes from digging up the corpses. Just as night fell, they gathered round the graves and bowed their heads. No-Head, not removing his hat, recited as much of the Lord's Prayer as he could remember, then sang a short verse to the same tune as he sang to settle the steers:

> As I was a-walking out early in Texas,
> Dark was the morning and cold was the day,
> Who should I spy but one of my children,
> Draped in a blanket as cold as the clay . . .

'It's 'bout th' bes' I can do,' he said self-effacingly, 'my not bein' a churchified man m'self.'

Chapter 9

★

ONE-HOUSE
TOWN

Perryman's trading post seemed, from a distance, to be an unprepossessing place. The building itself was low and oblong with square shuttered windows and a wide porch, all under a sod roof. Nearby was a barn and a large fenced corral in the centre of which stood a lone black walnut tree. Smoke seeped through the sod to such an extent that the whole building looked like a charcoal-maker's fire. In the immediate vicinity of the post were a dozen or so tents, a number of wagons drawn up into a defensive circle and a line of horses tethered to a rope stretched between two posts. Around the wagons, several children were playing with a hoop and skipping rope while, on the frame of one wagon, laundry hung out to dry. Close by, a young woman was rinsing her hair in a bucket of water. A cooking fire burned in the centre of the circle, tended by three other women wearing poke bonnets and aprons.

No-Head, ordering the herd to be kept back a way, rode ahead with Daniel and entered the trading post.

After the bright sunlight outside, the interior was dark and cool, despite the fact that a large, square stove in the middle was alight with a pot of coffee simmering to one side of the hot plate. Smoke leaked from a split in the chimney above it. Behind a counter were ranged shelves laden with all manner of provisions and supplies: dried bison meat, long-bladed knives in leather sheathes, cooking implements, dried fruits, round cheeses wrapped in muslin, cans of oysters, pots of preserved jams, cakes of pemmican, hardtack, strings of onions and bright red chillies, bottles of lime juice, bags of sugar and salt, tins of kerosene, lanterns, candles, bolts of cloth and items of clothing. Barrels and sacks of flour, cornmeal and potatoes stood on the floor beneath them along with buckets, shovels and picks, boxes of ammunition of various calibres, coils of rope and squares of tarpaulin or canvas. Leaning back in a chair was a man wearing a slouch hat and smoking a corncob pipe. At several tables men sat together, conversing in low tones, with mugs of coffee or ale before them. As Daniel and No-Head entered, everyone fell silent. The man with the pipe tipped his chair forward and got to his feet, hitching his pants up as he did so.

'How do, travellers?' he greeted them.

No-Head touched the brim of his hat; Daniel removed his.

'We're doin' fine, thank y', Mr Perryman,' replied No-Head.

'You know me, sir?' Perryman said with a hint of suspicion.

'I come through a while back,' No-Head answered noncommittally.

Perryman looked hard at him for a minute, then said, 'I remember you. You're th' one what's got a hole in his head.'

As he spoke, everyone looked at No-Head.

'That's me,' No-Head admitted. 'Scalped an' skimmed but still standin' an' talkin'. An' shootin' if needs be.'

'And my name's Daniel,' said Daniel.

'So, where're y' from?' Perryman asked.

'San Antone, heading north,' Daniel replied.

'North's a big place. Got a destination in mind?' Perryman went on.

Daniel and No-Head exchanged looks. Both instinctively knew it was best not to say too much, give too much away.

'Just north,' Daniel replied. 'We're driving fifty head north.'

'Fifty head,' Mr Perryman repeated contemplatively. 'With that many beeves, I'd say you was makin' for Kansas City.'

'Could be,' No-Head replied noncommittally.

'Then what confuses me is that you two southerners is headin' f' a beehive of true Blue

Bellies,' Perryman remarked, 'an' no mistake.'

'A what?' asked No-Head after a moment's silence.

'Blue Bellies. Whole area 'round there's taken by 'em. Anyone even flying a Confederate flag up there gets int' a pile o' trouble. They's built 'em a fort, too. Called it Camp Union. Elected a new mayor, a Liberationist, an' now he's been made a major in th' Missouri Militia. Wants to free all the slaves.'

No-Head went to the stove and poured two mugs of coffee, adding a spoonful of molasses to each and handing one to Daniel. This done, he tossed a coin to Mr Perryman, who caught it and put it in a pouch hanging from his waist.

'Much 'bliged,' the trader said.

Side by side, they sat at one of the tables.

'If this's all true,' No-Head said in a quiet voice, 'we could be in f' a hitch or two. I'm pretty sure Matt wouldn't've wanted us selling th' beeves t' th' Blue Bellies, but it looks like we got us no choice. We can hardly take 'em back. By th' time we reach Dark Creek they'd be jus' hide an' bone. They's skinny enough now t' need a bit o' fattening b'fore we sells them as it is.'

Four men detached themselves from a group talking in one corner to sit next to No-Head, who nodded a greeting to them. Daniel moved along the bench to make room for them.

'Y'all been travellin' long?' one of the men enquired.

'Six, maybe seven weeks,' admitted Daniel.

'Come 'cross any trouble?' The man's tone of voice suggested that he anticipated the answer.

'A Choctaw tried t' steal one of th' horses,' No-Head said, 'but we seed 'im off. How 'bout you?'

The men looked from one to the other, as if not sure whether to admit what had happened to them. Finally, a man in a check shirt and duck trousers spoke up.

'We're headin' west,' he said, 'headin' for th' moun'ains. Aim to set us up a town there in th' name of th' Lord. But 'bout seventy miles east of here we was jumped by this band of men. Fifteen, maybe twenty of them. Armed to th' teeth they were. Had more weapons than th' armies of God.'

'Blue Bellies?' ventured No-Head.

'No, sir,' came the reply. 'But they had officers jus' like an army. We'd been warned o' 'em. People say they calls themselves Quantrill's Raiders. Ain't hard t' tell who they is or isn't b'cause some of 'em wear a red sash 'round their belts. They ain't Blue Bellies an' they ain't Confed'rates, though they side with the Rebs. They's in-between an' they don't give a choice damn who they kill so long's there's somethin' in it for 'em.'

No-Head thoughtfully sipped at his coffee.

'Did you lose anyone?' Daniel asked.

'They split us up. One wagon ain't come in yet.'

'A wife, a husband and a little girl?' Daniel enquired.

'Ted and Abigail Scupham an' their little tyke, Joely. All three good Quaker folk.'

No-Head removed his hat out of respect. All the men raised their eyes looking for the hole in his head and saw the dent in the top of his cranium.

'I'm sorry t' report,' No-Head said, 'that we buried 'em a couple of days back. Leastways, th' adults. Th' child fell out th' wagon while they was bein' chased.'

No-Head put his hat back on. The men at the table fell silent then rose to their feet, leaving the trading post. A few minutes later, Daniel and No-Head heard the singing of a doleful hymn coming from the direction of the circle of wagons.

'Mr Perryman,' Daniel said, walking to the counter, 'we would be greatly obliged if you would permit us to stay nearby for a while. If the raiders are still in the area, there might be safety in numbers.'

'That's fine by me,' said Mr Perryman, 'on condition you buys what supplies 're needed from me while you're stayin' here.'

By night, the herd was kept in one of Mr Perryman's three corrals, being taken out in the daytime to graze on the range. For the use of the corral, Mr Perryman charged fifty cents per day, which No-Head considered extortionate in the extreme on account of the fact that no fodder was provided.

However, No-Head paid the price, saying, 'When

it comes down to it, we ain't got no alternative. When th' devil's got y' by th' tail, y' jus' jump when he decides an' forget dancin' to yer own pipe.'

When he wasn't riding circle, Daniel spent time cleaning his Navy Colt, dubbining his saddle and bridle, combing Satan's mane and tail and checking his hooves for any sharp stones that might have lodged there. Everyone took it in turn to help Jesus prepare meals and tidy the camp wagon. After the crossing of the Canadian River, the vehicle was in need of repair. Swinging it over the water had weakened the wheel mountings when they had struck the bank sideways on. The brace at the rear required particular attention. No-Head noticed it had begun to split and he was doubtful it would last out the rest of the journey to Kansas City. It was his opinion that it needed to be strengthened with a metal band but there was no forge at Perryman's place. Besides, Daniel had a better idea.

'Why don't we just carve a new brace?' he suggested.

'Easier said than done,' replied No-Head.

'Th' only wood round here hard enough for a

reach brace is hickory. An' that makes it too hard t' carve with th' tools we got with us. It ain't soft, like mountain pine,' Trinity observed.

Daniel smiled knowingly and set off north on Satan, carrying a saw borrowed from Perryman. He returned just before dusk with a six-foot length of hickory dragging behind him.

The next morning, they jacked the camp wagon up, took out the iron cotter pins and removed the rear wheels to give them better access to the underside of the vehicle. As No-Head removed the split reach brace, it snapped in two, one half falling to the ground.

'I sure hope you know what you's doin',' he said tersely to Daniel. 'If y' don't, we'll be here to see the snows come down.'

All through the morning, Daniel worked on the length of hickory, shaping it to match the old brace. This he did by carefully charring small sections of the wood with a large, bone-handled marlinspike heated in a fire. Trinity kept the flames well supplied with kindling, blowing the embers and raising the spike to white-hot with a small pair of bellows loaned by one of the homesteaders. Controlling the burning and removing the black charcoal with his knife, Daniel made sure all the while that the new brace was identical to the old, which he used as a template. The smoke itched his eyes and made his clothes smell of ash. When noon came, he continued working, breaking neither for food nor a *siesta*.

Finally, in the early afternoon, he paused. Beto brought him a large jug of water which he drank in one, finishing it off with a satisfied belch.

'It's done,' Daniel declared, standing up and easing his back muscles.

The reach brace was a perfect fit onto the wagon, the bolt holes Daniel had burned through with the white-hot spike measuring up precisely with the ones left by the previous piece. Replacing the wheels, No-Head greased them with rendered fat and gradually slid them into position. At about four o'clock, the camp wagon was lowered to the ground. Jesus backed the dray horses into the tongue of the wagon, attached the traces to them and set off down the track. For the first hundred yards, the wheels squeaked but then fell silent and ran smoothly.

'How in th' name of God's creation did you know t' work wood like that?' No-Head asked Daniel with a hint of wonderment in his voice.

'My father taught me,' Daniel replied. 'He was a carpenter and wheelwright. In England he used beech when he needed hard wood, but I reckoned the hickory was no different.'

Considering its remoteness, Daniel was surprised that so many people knew of Perryman's trading post. Each day, he would return from riding circle as the herd grazed to find one or two new horses tethered outside the store and, inside, their owners engaged in business with Perryman or swapping stories and news across a mug of coffee. Joining them, No-Head would frequently turn the conversation to Quantrill's Raiders, discovering that it was believed they were still in the area. It was on account of this threat that many of the people chose to camp for a while at the trading post rather than travel on.

As No-Head philosophically stated, 'Better safety in numbers.'

'Never a truer word was spoke,' commented one burly man, a buffalo-hunter who carried a rifle of such a calibre that Daniel wondered how any man could fire it and absorb the recoil. 'They's got three men ridin' with 'em as was spawned by the devil himself, I swears t' God. Two brothers, go by the name of James. Jesse and Frank. Meaner than a bear with his foot in a snare. T'other's a mean highbinder by th' name of Cole Younger. Killin's a sport for th' three of 'em. They'd ride down a man jus' as keen as they would a coyote.'

Within a few days of the arrival of the Dark Creek herd, Perryman's post could count amongst its residents six trappers, who had ridden in towing two sledges laden with assorted pelts, an itinerant preacher in a grimy soutane and a patent medicine salesman, as well as the homesteaders.

Needless to say, this pleased Mr Perryman and his two sons, George and Josiah, who helped him run the trading post. The more who stayed over, the more they profited.

On the afternoon of his fourth day at Perryman's place, as Daniel was tending to Satan, an apparition rode up to the trading post.

He was a tall man riding a handsome chestnut Arab stallion. Draped from his shoulders was a long, black frock coat. His white shirt had a lace collar with more lace flounced at the cuffs. His ensemble was finished off with a flat-crowned, wide-brimmed hat and black boots of tooled Mexican leather. His hair was shoulder-length, blond and wavy. Tied to his saddlehorn was a carpetbag with a polished brass catch. As he dismounted from his horse, Daniel caught sight of two pistols at his side, their grips inlaid with ivory.

Beto also saw him arrive and walked over to Daniel.

'You mus' have care, *señorito*,' Beto said, his voice low. 'This man is . . .' He searched in vain for words in English to express his thoughts. 'A man in such cloths is . . . You may be sure he is *pistoliero*.'

Fascinated by both man and mount, Daniel approached the horse and stared at it.

'May I be of some assistance to you, young sir?' the man asked.

His accent was cultured, not that of a *vaquero* or, Daniel thought, even of an American. He also spoke in a measured fashion, as if taking care over every word he uttered. His blue eyes seemed to bore into Daniel's.

Taken aback at being spoken to, Daniel made no immediate reply so the man gathered up his carpet-bag, turned and entered the trading post.

As evening fell, No-Head and Trinity returned with the herd, guiding them into the corral for the night. As the last steers passed through the gate, No-Head saw the stallion tethered with the other horses.

'Goldarn it!' he exclaimed with more than a hint of admiration. 'I seed me some fine horses in my time, but that! Reckon a king'd ride a horse that purdy. Did y' see who brung it in?'

Daniel described the man.

No-Head was momentarily thoughtful then set off towards the trading post, Daniel and Trinity following him.

'I rec'mend keepin' an eye on this one. A man

carryin' pieces such as you describe, Daniel, 's sure
t' be a shootist.'

By now, darkness had fallen and the building was
full of men seated at the tables or on benches round
the stove. Some were Creek Indians, friends of Mr
Perryman who was himself half Creek. One in
particular caught Daniel's attention. He was elderly,
tall and thin with an aquiline nose. His face was
creased by wrinkles, his skin as tanned as leather
and his eyes watery and vague. He sat alone,
hunched up at the end of a bench, his long greying
hair tied back. On his head was an old top hat in the
band of which was fixed an eagle's feather.

'Who is he?' Trinity asked No-Head.

'His name's Sees Far,' No-Head replied quietly.
'They say he can see better than a man with a
tel'scope.'

The old Indian got to his feet and put his arm out
to rest his hand on Trinity's shoulder, his fingers
gripping her like a bird's talons. She jumped.

'I hears far, too, little girlie,' the Indian muttered
in a gruff deep voice, yet he was smiling, 'I hears the
cricket talkin' in a high storm.'

The air was thick with wood and tobacco smoke, which was marbled by the light of the lamps. The conversation centred mainly on the weather, the lie of the land to the west, news of the war and the possible proximity of Quantrill's Raiders, whom the preacher had come across two days before.

Standing by the stove and warming his hands, Daniel surveyed the gathering, looking for the owner of the Arab stallion. He was sitting on his own in a corner, his back to the wall, his chair tilted back on its legs, his feet on the crossbar of the table before him on which stood a silver hip flask. In his hand he held a small engraved crystal glass half-full of amber liquid. In the heat of the room, Daniel could smell the delicate fumes of an expensive bourbon. He touched No-Head's sleeve and slightly inclined his head in the man's direction.

No-Head collected three mugs of coffee from the stove and walked over to the man's table with Daniel and Trinity.

'You mind if we plan' ourselves down here?' No-Head asked.

The man shrugged. No-Head, Daniel and

Trinity settled themselves down opposite him.

'Fine horse you got out there,' No-Head remarked in passing, sipping at his coffee. 'That an Ay-rab?'

'It could be,' came the reply.

'You sure didn't buy him roun' here,' No-Head continued. 'You get 'im out east?'

'Maybe.' The man put his whiskey glass to his lips then lowered it halfway to the table. 'If you don't mind my observing,' he continued, 'you are an exceedingly curious man.'

The words were urbane and polite and yet simultaneously somehow laden with threat. Daniel felt unaccountably uneasy. Trinity touched his hand as if seeking some kind of reassurance: she, too, felt the terror in this man's company. However, despite this, Daniel could not help but notice the man's accent.

'Pardon me, sir, but are you English?' Daniel asked.

The man looked up, lowered his feet to the floor and, leaning forward, ran his eyes over Daniel.

'And who might be asking?'

'My name is Daniel Chance,' admitted Daniel.

No-Head and Trinity exchanged glances, wondering what else they might now learn about the boy who had arrived at Dark Creek on a stolen *burro*.

'Well!' exclaimed the man. 'Fancy my hearing an English voice this far beyond the horizons of civilized persons. And from where might you hail, Mr Chance?'

'The county of Kent,' Daniel replied. 'And what's your name, sir?'

The man paused for a moment before answering.

'My name,' he said at length, 'is Arthur James Maugham, gentleman of the county of Hampshire in the realm of Her Majesty Queen Victoria, although the ragamuffins of the erstwhile colonies of America choose to refer to me otherwise.' He held his hand out. 'I'm pleased to make your acquaintance, sir.'

Daniel shook the proffered hand. The skin was soft but the hold firm.

At the mention of the man's name, one of the trappers murmured, 'It's Lond'n Jim.'

Everyone fell silent.

187

'Indeed, gentleman,' James Maugham announced, standing up and bowing, 'your company is blessed by the presence of London Jim. And you, Master Chance, what brings you to Indian country?'

'I am a *vaquero*,' Daniel replied proudly.

'So it would seem from your garb. You would not be picking hops in the fields of Kent so dressed. Yet that is no answer, young sir. But fair is fair, Master Chance. You have your story but you'll play it close. The best way, I assure you, and I respect that.' He turned to No-Head. 'And you are . . . ?'

'Nolan,' No-Head replied.

'An Irish name if I'm not mistaken,' London Jim said. 'What's your game, Mister Nolan? Other than driving beeves, that is.'

'Poker,' No-Head answered abruptly.

London Jim reached into his jacket pocket and produced a small silver box. Snapping it open, he withdrew a well-worn deck of cards, their backs red but their edges brown with the dirt and sweat of many players' hands.

'Can I offer you a game, Mr Nolan? What do you say?' London Jim asked.

'I'd not be impartial,' No-Head answered.

Daniel realized this was probably why No-Head had joined London Jim at his table. It seemed gambling men had a knack for recognizing one another.

'Would any of you gentleman care to pass the pastes with us?' London Jim called out, addressing the trappers across the room. Two of them came to the table, followed by the preacher.

Perryman stepped out from behind the store counter. 'Gentlemen,' he said, 'I don't mind gamblin' in my place but I must insist I hold your pieces. So unbuckle your gun belts if you will. I'll put 'em out back an' you can have 'em back when all's done an' finished. Josiah, George, collect 'em up an' lock 'em in th' chest.'

'I am not averse,' London Jim declared, handing over his ivory-handled revolvers to Perryman's sons, 'but I'll retain my belt if I may, for the sake of decorum.' He nodded in Trinity's direction. 'There is, I see, a lady in the company and I would be loath to drop my pants in such a presence. Even here, beyond the farthest reaches of gentility, standards must be retained.'

No-Head and the two trappers did as they were instructed as well.

'And you, preacher . . . ?' Mr Perryman added.

'As a man of God, I abjure carrying a firearm,' the preacher said portentously but he still handed in a small pocket Derringer, adding, 'For protection from wild beasts on the trail.'

'Hope y' don't meet a grizzly, preacher,' No-Head remarked. 'That'll give him no more'n a tickle.'

'You too, boy,' Perryman went on, addressing Daniel. 'You might not be playin' but you're ridin' with Mr No-Head here.'

Daniel reluctantly took off his gun belt and handed it to Josiah Perryman.

'If you concur, gentlemen,' said London Jim, 'the game is poker, five-card draw.'

London Jim dealt the first hand, the cards sliding across the table as if on a surface of glass. No-Head collected his cards but, rather than pick them up off the table, he just bent a corner up so far as he could see what cards he held.

It was not many hands before Daniel realized that

London Jim was an expert player. The preacher, on the other hand, was weak, occasionally touching the wooden cross that hung around his neck on a cord, inadvertently signalling to the other players that he was bluffing. The trappers were more skilled but still lost, neither of them being up to the calibre of London Jim or No-Head, whose piles of Union silver dollars and Confederate notes grew steadily on the table before them. At the start of the game, No-Head had pulled the brim of his hat down to cover his eyes. London Jim sat motionless and expressionless, moving only to shuffle or deal the cards, bet, sort his hand or drink from his whiskey glass, which he refilled every so often from his flask. No one spoke except to name their bet or declare their hand.

An hour and a half into the poker game, No-Head hit a losing streak. For six consecutive hands, he bet strongly only to have the game go to London Jim.

'You appear to have hit a dry run. Do you wish to continue, sir?' London Jim asked No-Head.

No-Head nodded and said, 'I'd like th'

opp'rtun'ty t' win back some of my losin's.'

London Jim dealt the next hand. No-Head briefly studied his cards and put five silver dollars in the centre of the table.

'Call!' said London Jim quietly and he bet likewise.

No-Head discarded two cards and London Jim dealt him two replacements. As No-Head reached for his new cards, London Jim stood up, rocking the table, his hip flask falling on its side, spilling the remains of its contents. His chair fell back against the wall. Leaning forward with one hand on the table, London Jim looked straight at No-Head.

'Do you take me for a fool, sir?' he muttered through clenched teeth. 'I would beg to inform you, a mere rustic, that I have been playing the Mississippi and Rio Grande riverboats and I know a sharp when I see one.'

Everyone turned and watched as No-Head slowly raised the brim of his hat with one finger and got to his feet.

'An' I knows a thievin', cheatin' son of a bitch when I sees one,' No-Head replied.

Out of the corner of his eye, Daniel saw a card slide from No-Head's cuff into the stack of cards on the table.

'You, sir,' London Jim answered, 'will live to eat those words, but not much longer.'

No-Head looked at the planks of the floor by London Jim's feet. Following his gaze, Daniel could see a card on the floor under the table. It was the Queen of Spades.

'That,' No-Head suggested, pointing to the floor, 'might not be th' portrait of your own dear Queen Victoria, might it?'

A faint smile spread across London Jim's face. He picked up his flask. Swallowing back the last few drops of liquor left in it, he screwed the top back on. Opening his jacket with his left hand, London Jim replaced the flask in an inside pocket, his hand sliding down to his gun belt under the cover of his coat. Daniel wondered for a moment if the Englishman had forgotten he no longer carried a gun. When his hand returned to view, it held a thin stiletto, the blade shining dully in the light of the lamps. With the agility of an angry cat, his arm lashed out but No-Head was too quick for him. He blocked the attack, grabbing London Jim's hand, bending it back and under at the wrist. Daniel heard the Englishman's joints crack. The stiletto fell to the table.

London Jim broke from No-Head's grip and took up the dagger again. Getting a firm hold on No-Head's coat, he yanked it towards him, pulling him over the table. Then, raising his hand above his head, he readied to plunge the knife into No-Head's back.

No-Head swung himself to one side, the knife missing his arm by a matter of inches. He lashed out at London Jim's face, his blow catching him on the right cheek. London Jim was momentarily knocked off balance but did not lose his grip on his knife or No-Head's clothing.

'Drop th' knife, sir,' came a voice from behind Daniel. The words were accompanied by a metallic click.

Daniel turned. Standing by his shoulder was Trinity, her four-shot pepperbox pistol held out at arm's length, pointed directly at London Jim's head. The weapon was cocked.

194

'Well! Well!' London Jim remarked, putting the knife back in its hiding place in his gun belt. 'Observe Master Chance how, beyond the borders of accepted society, one must beware even of slips of girls.'

'And cheats,' Daniel added.

'When in Rome, dear young sir,' London Jim retorted, 'do as the Romans do.' He addressed No-Head. 'I suggest, sir, we let this event pass as a slight *contretemps* between our respective nations.'

There was another, firmer, click behind Daniel. He looked over his shoulder to see Perryman and his two sons holding levelled shotguns.

'I'll abide no trouble here,' said Perryman. 'As for you, little lady . . .'

'You didn't ask me for my gun, Mr Perryman,' Trinity said, sweetly. She uncocked the pepperbox, felt under her skirts and secreted it away.

'Would you have used your little toy-gun, sweet child?' London Jim enquired.

'You'll never know, Mister Jim,' Trinity answered. 'An' you should not enquire. You're a card player. If you want t' call a bluff, you has to pay.'

195

London Jim started laughing, the other men joining in. The atmosphere in the trading post lightened.

'Come sun-up,' Mr Perryman ordered, 'I wants y'all off my prop'ty an' ridin' out for wherever it is you's headin'.' He and his sons uncocked their shotguns. 'You get your weapons returned in the mornin'. An',' he went on, 'you returns the money you two took off these trappers an' th' preacher-man. They ain't rich men.'

No-Head put twelve silver dollars on the table, London Jim twenty-two. The trappers scooped up the coins.

'Let this be a lesson unto you,' pontificated the preacher. 'Associating with the Devil's henchmen'll cost you dear. So sayeth I—'

'Shut your maw, preacher,' snapped one of the trappers. 'I don't see you returnin' none of my lucre what you took with three of a kin'.'

'What need have I for money?' the preacher rejoined. 'I am wealthy in the glory of the Lord. My rewards shall come.' Yet he still took his share of the gaming money.

As they walked back to the camp wagon, Daniel asked No-Head, 'You were cheating, weren't you? I saw you slip a card . . .'

'Once I knowed he was,' No-Head confirmed. 'An' that was from th' very start.'

'Did you win Satan by cheating as well?' Daniel went on.

'No, there was no need,' No-Head replied. 'I won 'im fair an' square, but ol' Satan's owner was a real bad player. Truth be, Satan was smarter by half than his owner. Yet I've sat at enough poker tables t' know when there's someone tryin' it on. I saw that London Jim playin' a line right from the beginnin'. I could've called him out, but th' only way to see a cheat without your gun belt on's t' cheat yourself.'

Daniel considered this for a moment. 'So you're saying that two wrongs make a right?'

'Out here,' No-Head answered enigmatically, 'two wrongs can make a pumpkin pie for all I cares. Nobody gets a rise out o' No-Head Nolan.'

Chapter 10

★

QUANTRILL'S RAIDERS

All morning, the air had been oppressive. The steers plodded on slowly, their heads hung low, their hooves kicking up a cloud of dust that hung in the windless air. Occasionally, one would low, the others taking up the mournful sound. Daniel rode at the head of the herd, keeping a keen lookout for anyone who might be in their path. At mid-morning, they came upon a small Chickasaw settlement consisting of half a dozen tepees. As they passed it by, a number of children came out to peer at them. The womenfolk stood in a huddle by a frame upon which was stretched a bison hide. Nearby, a wooden rack held lengths of meat drying in the sun. An elderly man dressed in an embroidered buckskin jacket, a tight cloth band wound around his head, surveyed their passage and raised his hand in salute. No-Head returned the greeting and called out, 'Halito!' A brief conversation ensued of which Daniel did not understand a single word.

Not far from the tepees were several cultivated patches of beans, squash and corn. Daniel positioned himself along the edge so as to prevent the steers from entering and damaging the crops.

Gradually, as the herd moved on, the distant sky began to fill with dense clouds. Yet they were not dark grey like those of an impending weather front or thunderstorm but looked, to Daniel, to be dun brown in colour, almost a sort of khaki. The hue reminded him of English clouds of impending snow; perhaps, he reasoned, this was a hailstorm approaching.

A few minutes later, as if to give substance to his thoughts, something hit hard on the brim of his hat.

Next, something struck Satan between the ears and bounced onto his mane. It was not a pebble of ice. It was a large green and brown grasshopper about the size of Daniel's little finger.

No-Head galloped up.

'Cover y' face, tuck y' sleeves in y' gloves, pull y' hat brim down! We're in for it.'

'What is it?' Daniel shouted back.

'Hopper storm,' No-Head yelled over an increasing hizzing noise that seemed to emanate from the very air around them. 'An' they got spines on their legs.'

Daniel tugged his bandanna up to just below his eyes. No sooner had he done so than the cloud descended and the air became thick with grasshoppers. They struck Daniel's jacket, ricocheted off his boots, landed on Satan's neck and in the horse's ears. He shook his head violently to dislodge them.

The air was filled with the shrill whisper of millions of insect wings. One grasshopper, landing on Daniel's bandanna, got under it and onto his chin, crawling up towards his mouth. He swatted it, its intestines bursting out of its abdomen to smear his lips. They tasted bitter. He felt the bile rise in his throat and fought it back.

The steers broke into a trot.

'Hold 'em back!' No-Head shouted above the zizzing din. 'Don't let 'em break!'

Yet it was too late; the steers were running now, trying to evade the blizzard of grasshoppers which became all the more dense. Daniel narrowed his eyes. Satan drew level with the front runners and tried to turn them, edging into their path, ever conscious of their huge, sharp horns. Yet the steers would not be deflected from their mission to escape the insects, some of which tried to climb into their ears and nostrils.

Just as suddenly as it had arrived, the cloud vanished and the ground was a seething carpet of insects. They clung to every twig and blade of grass, every branch of every bush, their tiny mandibles chewing any vegetation they could find. The sound of their wings was replaced by the hideous sound of their feeding.

Daniel nudged Satan into a gallop, horse and

rider racing as one along the side of the herd. Not far to Daniel's left rode Beto. As his horse's hooves plunged down, they sent up small clouds of grasshoppers. Beneath Satan's hooves Daniel could hear the crackle of hundreds of grasshoppers being stomped to pulp. The steers' hooves pounded on the hard, dry ground.

It took a mile to stop the herd. Just as they were coming to a halt, the grasshoppers took to the wing. In less than a minute, they were gone, whirring up as one to form another cloud in the sky which drifted towards the horizon with a diminishing sizz. All around the herd, there was not a green plant to be seen, with the exception of the prickly pear cactuses.

'I feels for them Indians,' No-Head remarked as they set off once more. 'Them 'hoppers'll'ave eaten th' crops t' sticks. It'll be a hard winter for 'em, like as not. Guess they'll be eatin' cactus till the spines come out through their hides.'

'What about their horses?' Daniel asked.

'They'll ride 'em off to some pasture beyond the swarm's reach or they'll feed 'em cactus. An' before

you ask,' No-Head said, 'they pile straw round th'
cactus bush, put a fire to it an' burn off th' spines.
Same for th' steers if there's a drought.'

At sundown, they set up camp in an outcrop of
large boulders. While Jesus got a cook fire going
and Beto settled the herd down for the night in a
large open grassy space amongst the boulders,
Daniel climbed onto one of the huge rocks and sat
down. On the flat face of the stone opposite him
were Indian pictograms of stick men hunting bison
and bear with bows and spears, some of them per-
forming in what appeared to be a ritual dance.
When the daylight faded, so did the pictograms, as
if they were stepping back into ancient history. The
first stars shone brightly in the sky, pricks of silver
against the deep azure of the coming night.

'See that one?' Trinity asked, clambering up the
rock to sit next to Daniel.

'Which?'

'That real bright one.' She pointed to it. 'That's
called Venus. An' that' – she pointed again – 'that
red un's Mars. They say that un's nearer to Earth
than all th' others.' She swept her hand across the

heavens, as if she was casting stardust over the night.

'Who told you all this?' Daniel enquired.

'They got a teacher in D'Hanis. He tol' me. He knows all kind o' things.'

'Do you go to school?' Daniel asked in amazement.

'Hell, no!' Trinity answered. 'I tried it one time but it didn't fit me good and, b'sides, I didn't learn me much. My parents teach me most things I need to know. My ma teached me sewing an' they sure as hell don' teach you how to load a Colt in the classroom. As for cookin', Jesus taught me. ''ve you bin t' school?'

'I went to school in England.'

'What was that like?' Trinity asked with more than a hint of curiosity.

'Well it was . . .' Daniel had to search for the words. 'It was just school. All the children had to go into a building by the church.'

'What was it made of?'

'Stone.'

'And the roof?' Trinity asked.

'The roof was made of slate.'

'Slate? What's slate?'

'Well,' Daniel explained, 'slate's thin sheets of stone they cut from the block. It's very shiny when it rains and sometimes when a big bird, like a crow, lands on it they can't get hold and slide down.' He smiled at the memory of the rooks from the elm trees in the graveyard careering down the wet slates to land in a flapping, dishevelled and undignified pile in the tall grass between the headstones.

'What did they teach you in school?' Trinity wanted to know.

'Well, they taught me to read and write and do arithmetic.'

'What's 'rithm'tick?'

'Well, it's . . .' Daniel explained. 'Well it's adding up and subtracting and multiplication and division.'

Trinity looked at him with wide eyes. 'Why! You mean you can do all that fancy stuff with numbers?'

Daniel nodded.

Somewhere far off on the prairie came the whirring of a nighthawk's wings.

'D' y' think you could teach me some of that?'

'Certainly,' said Daniel. 'It's not very difficult.' He looked to the horizon. There were several brief flashes of light low down in the sky. A few moments later, they were followed by a sound like muffled thunder.

'You of a mind that's guns?' Trinity thought aloud. ''s th' war 'gainst the North comin' closer?'

'I don't think so,' Daniel answered. 'It's just heat lightning.'

Suddenly, there was a gash of light across the sky.

'You see that?' Trinity exclaimed.

'It was a shooting star,' Daniel said.

'I knowed that,' Trinity replied defensively. 'I ain't that dumb.'

'I didn't mean to say you were,' Daniel said.

'Just 'cause I don't know my tables nor nothing, don't mean I ain't got anything in my head.'

'I know,' said Daniel. 'You've got much more in your head about steers and horses and guns and living in wild places and the Karakawa than I could ever have.'

'That's right,' Trinity replied. 'An' don't you forget it!'

Daniel felt as if he had been thoroughly put in his place, but Trinity was smiling. She slid down the boulder, Daniel watching her dark shape moving off towards the camp wagon in the starlight. The camp-fire glimmered on the rocks, a faint drift of smoke rising into the sky. The pictograms seemed to dance in the darkness like ghost stick puppets.

'You comin' t' eat?' Trinity called back. ''s near ready.'

'Shortly,' Daniel answered.

He leaned back on his arms and gazed into the sky, waiting for yet another meteor to streak across it.

As dawn broke, the sky was a cover of high clouds which Daniel knew would soon burn off when the sun rose. The herd stood quietly in a clearing of tall grass surrounded by thick brush.

Throughout the night, Daniel had let Satan have his head. The horse knew what was expected of him and walked at a steady pace around the herd, keeping to the perimeter of the brush. Daniel had let his body sway to the rhythm of the horse's gait and, intermittently, softly sang *Greensleeves* to the steers.

Remembering the tune saddened Daniel. His mother had sung it as a lullaby for his sister as she lay dying of smallpox: and now, he thought, he was doing likewise to a herd of longhorns in a strange land. Yet, he further considered, it was no longer so strange. It was becoming a part of him, and he a part of it.

In the weak early daylight, the steers at one end of the clearing began to grow restless. One after another, they turned to face a patch of dense scrub and cactus, snuffling at the air, tossing their heads, knocking their horns together and pawing the ground. Roja, who had been sauntering along in front of Satan for an hour or so, sniffing at rabbit holes and swinging his leg against bushes and cacti, suddenly froze. His hackles rose and he started to growl deep in his throat.

Daniel turned Satan in that direction, loosening his Navy Colt in its holster that hung against his thigh. The horse progressed for a short distance, then stopped ten paces from Roja. Daniel tapped his heels in against the horse's ribs.

'Walk on, Satan,' he half-whispered, leaning forward to the horse's ear.

Yet Satan would not move. Instead, the horse raised his head, shook his mane and gently whinnied. Through the saddle and saddle blanket, Daniel felt his mount begin to tremble.

'Walk on,' Daniel repeated.

Satan adamantly stood his ground.

Daniel studied the cover closely. Nothing was moving. Not so much as a bird hopped from twig to twig.

He ran over the possibilities in his mind: Indians? – hardly likely to spook the steers and especially Satan; a rattler? – it was still too cold and early in the morning for reptiles which, Daniel knew, had to be warmed by the sun before becoming active. So, what?

It was then Daniel saw something in the deep dawn shadow of a bush. It was about as long as he was tall, a light tawny brown in colour, almost grey.

At one end was a long tail, at the other a cat's head. Its mouth was open and Daniel could see a pair of sharp incisors. As he watched, the black tip of the tail began to twitch and its ears flattened. Then, with a movement that he almost could not follow with his eye, the creature was up and bounding towards Roja on the edge of the herd.

'Roja!' Daniel yelled, tugging the Navy Colt clear if its holster.

The dog turned. Daniel's shout momentarily took the predator's attention but it pressed home its attack, leaping onto Roja's back, seeking to get his neck in its jaws.

Satan started to weave and buck. Daniel aimed the revolver as best he could and fired. The lead slug hit the creature in the side, the impact knocking it off Roja. Yet the creature's claws were sunk in the dog's flesh and he too was bowled over.

Daniel fired again. The shot missed its target and struck the earth beyond, the ricochet whining into the air with a brief, high-pitched drone.

The dawn air grew dusty as the steers jinxed, scattering to escape the gunfire and commotion.

The pounding of horses' hooves signalled the arrival of the others. No-Head pulled his Spencer rifle from its scabbard and fired, hardly bothering to aim the weapon. The cat rolled over, dead, a bleeding hole in the side of its ribcage.

Trinity rode up at a gallop, reined her horse in and ran to Roja. The dog had been badly mauled, three strips of his skin hanging loose, showing a yellowish fat layer beneath. He was also bleeding from a wound on the back of his neck.

'What is it?' Daniel asked as he stood by the carcass of the cat.

'That there's a mount'n lion,' No-Head said, looking down at its body. 'Some folks calls it a cougar, others a painter or a catamount. Either ways, it's not t' be tangled with. You don't norm'lly see 'em,' he continued. 'They's shy, but when they got their courage up or they've a mind to a kill . . .'

'Why did it attack Roja?' Daniel asked.

'T' eat,' No-Head replied. 'Cougars take jack rabbits, *javelinas* an' such but they's also not impartial t' coyotes and dogs. I even heard of Indian children bein' killed.'

The injury in Roja's neck was bleeding profusely. They got him back to the camp wagon where, just as Fredo had when castrating the dogies back at Dark Creek, Beto took fresh wood ash from the campfire, scattering it over the wound and adding dried herbs from a leather pouch in his saddle roll and a drop of water to make a poultice which Jesus bound tightly round the wound. Trinity carefully replaced the hanging strips of torn skin and fur from Roja's back, sewing them in place with a needle and thread for all the world as if she were patching an old coat. Not once did the dog either wince or snap but just lay still as he was ministered to.

Beto set to skinning the mountain lion, cutting off its paws as souvenirs for Daniel and scraping the pelt clean, salting and rolling it up.

'What are those herbs you put on Roja's neck?' Daniel enquired, as Beto placed the pelt in the camp wagon.

'They are from the *curandero*,' Beto answered. 'How would you say? Like a doctor. He has much knowledge from many years ago.'

It took the better part of an hour to round up the scattered steers. By the time they were ready to roll them out again, the buzzards had eaten most of the mountain lion carcass. With Roja lying on a sack of straw in the back of the camp wagon, No-Head gave the signal and Trinity and Daniel positioned themselves behind the herd and shouted at the steers. Reluctantly, like children being made to set off for school on a rainy morning, the herd started to move forward.

Daniel and Satan mounted a small rise, where Daniel reined in his horse just below the skyline. Half a mile to his rear, the dust cloud kicked up by the steers drifted away from him, on a stiff breeze. Ahead was a range of low hills cut through by deep gullies devoid of vegetation. The landscape vaguely reminded Daniel of a privet maze he had once seen in Kent when helping his father deliver a five-bar gate to a rich landowner's country mansion.

Clambering onto a rock, he carefully surveyed the panorama. The hills ran for some fifteen miles east and west. To detour around them, he assessed, would add several days to the drive, days they could ill afford to lose. As No-Head had pointed out, the steers were underweight and the more word got out that cattle were fetching a good price in Kansas City, the more would be driven there and the lower the price would dip. As the navigator and guardian of Matt's maps and the compass, Daniel knew only too well that the responsibility to find a route through the hills fell to him.

Urging Satan into a canter, Daniel headed off towards the hills. Soon, he was riding through them, the rock walls towering fifty feet above him on either side. Using a wax pencil, Daniel sketched a rough plan of the passes as he rode. Several times he encountered dead-ends and had to back-track but he always made sure that he noted this on his map. This would be important information if they were to steer the herd through successfully.

After half an hour, Daniel felt that he must be near the other side of the hills and the discovery of a route through.

Rounding a corner in the pass, Daniel suddenly caught the smell of wood smoke drifting down

214

towards him from somewhere up ahead. As there was so little greenery in the valleys the smoke could not be coming from a natural fire: there must be people ahead. As No-Head and Beto were so far behind him, Daniel realized he would have to scout ahead by himself.

He dismounted Satan, tying his reins around a dead tree branch on the ground, and continued on by foot, gradually creeping towards the source of the smoke. Taking up position behind a large boulder, he quietly peered around it. Ahead, Daniel caught sight of a number of horses. He tried to count them but it was difficult to reach a precise number. The horses kept moving continually. They were uneasy. Beyond the horses was a campfire, over which hung a kettle supported by two sticks. Around the hearth Daniel could see three men talking, although he wasn't able to make out what they were saying over the snorting of the horses and the crackle of the flames. Suddenly, a fourth man appeared, walking to the fire from where he had been hidden from view behind the horses. Immediately, Daniel's eyes were drawn to the man's waist: around it, tied in a knot to one side, was a red sash.

Daniel's mouth went dry. He felt his heart begin to thump. He wanted to try to stop it, slow it down and silence it, but try as he might he could not. It seemed to him incredible that the men could not hear it, beating its tattoo in his chest.

Sliding back behind the boulder, he retreated as quickly as he could without making a noise or further spooking the horses. Reaching Satan, he leapt onto his back and rode out of the canyon as fast as the animal could take him, the map he had made ensuring that he did not take a wrong turn. Ten minutes later, he was back with the herd.

No-Head, seeing Daniel approaching so quickly, rode out to meet him.

'What's up, Daniel?' No-Head asked as Daniel and Satan slewed to a halt.

'In the hills ahead,' Daniel gasped, trying to catch his breath, 'camped up. It's Quantrill's Raiders!'

No-Head looked at Daniel. 'Y' sure?'

'Absolutely,' Daniel replied. 'I saw their red

sashes. I counted eighteen horses but can't be certain. There might be more.'

No-Head's face hardened. 'Well,' he said after a moment's consideration, 'I believe y' that they're Quantrill's Raiders. If y' counted eighteen horses, though, then maybe there's not so many of them as we might have feared. Some o' they horses will be f' carryin' food and equipment, not people. I reckon we's dealing with ten men, but this is still serious. If we carry on, they'll see the dust the steers're kicking up an' they'll be out here b'fore we know it. But I ain't turning round an' even if we detour there's a good chance we'd jus' see them on th' other side of them hills.'

No-Head thought for a moment longer, his gaze lifting to the hills ahead. Signalling for Daniel to follow him, No-Head turned his horse.

Pulling the herd up, he gathered Beto, Trinity and Jesus around him while he and Daniel described the situation.

'We can't fight ten killers,' Trinity said, her hand shaking as she held her horse's reins.

'That's true, we ain't goin' t' beat them in a

straight fight,' No-Head said. 'But we've somethin' they ain't got.'

'What?' she asked. 'Sure, we got guns. We got Spencers! But we ain't military trained. Them's crack soldiers.'

'What we got,' No-Head said, 'is they don't know we're here.' He looked from face to face of those around him: they did not look convinced. 'This is what we'll do: Trinity, you'll stay here an' watch th' steers. Beto, Jesus an' me'll hide at th' top of one of these dead-ends *arroyo*s Daniel's marked on his map. Then Daniel'll get their attention an' lead them to us. We'll spring 'em and take as many of them down as we can. Then we carry on to Kansas City. There's no guarantee, that's f' certain, but it's the best chance we got. We all agreed?'

'*Si*,' Beto said. 'It's crazy, but why not?'

Jesus voiced his assent. Daniel glanced at Trinity. He could tell she wasn't sure of No-Head's scheme but she nodded her approval all the same.

'Daniel?' No-Head asked.

'Yes,' Daniel said. 'I reckon we're only five or six days from Kansas City. After eight weeks on the trail already I'm not going to let a band of outlaws hold us up, whatever their reputation. And I reckon I can run faster than they can, though I'll have to take off my gun belt.'

'That's the kind of pluck I'm looking for!' No-Head exclaimed. 'It's true what they say about th' Brits. If we'd been up against the likes of you in the Revolutionary War, reckon th' president would still be wearing a crown and we'd be doffing our hats to a whole mess of colonial well-to-dos. Y' can leave your belt with Trinity. Now, let's go.'

Daniel took off his gun belt and handed it to Trinity, who rode off to circle the herd. Grabbing his rifle from the camp wagon, Jesus climbed up onto Beto's horse with him and the two of them, No-Head and Daniel rode off towards the hills.

Upon entering the first of the canyons, they stopped to consult Daniel's map.

'I remember that this end here has particularly steep sides,' Daniel said, pointing to the map. 'You should have a good line of sight to most of the valley floor. Also, it's not far from either Quantrill's Raiders' camp or the plain should we need to try and escape.'

'I agree with y', Daniel,' No-Head said. 'Y' give us fifteen minutes to get into position an' then y' know what t' do.'

Daniel nodded soberly and, studying the map one final time, handed it to No-Head. At that, No-Head and Beto, with Jesus behind him, turned their horses and rode away.

Daniel dismounted Satan, tying him up once more but this time well out of sight where he would be safe if matters were to take a turn for the worse. On foot, he now started to make his way along the route he had memorized through the canyons towards the camp. As he made his way along the dry canyon floor, his feet dislodged pebbles which rattled against each other as they fell into what were, when it rained, water courses. The sound echoed alarmingly, scaring a covey of bob-white quail which took flight with whirring wings. When he had ridden through before, Daniel had had Satan for company but now his fears rose inside him. Ahead lay a band of ruthless killers and, unarmed as he was, he had no way of protecting himself apart from by fleeing. Watching the quail veering from left to right in flight made him realize that he was going to have to do the same. His hands began to shake and his legs felt weak but he knew he had to continue.

Minutes later, he was crouching behind the same rock as he had previously, surveying the camp ahead of him. Again he counted eighteen horses, so at least no one had left or, more importantly, arrived since he was last there. Relaxing around the camp-fire he could still see four of Quantrill's Raiders. Two more were standing a little way to the left. No-Head was right, they did have the element of surprise.

Daniel waited. Not able to see the sun from the bottom of the canyon, he tried hard to concentrate on the passage of time. Finally, he decided, he must have given the others long enough to get into position. He breathed out deeply, trying to calm himself and then, sucking in a lungful of air, he stood up and ran out into the middle of the canyon. Nothing happened. They had not seen him.

Crouching, Daniel crept forward, leaning on his knuckles and keeping within the relative safety of the shadows of the rock walls. Every step he took was measured to ensure that he made as little sound as possible. Although he knew he had to attract their attention it was important to choose the right moment. He was lucky, he realized, that Quantrill's men did not have a dog. Even a dozy mutt like El Sueño would have given him away. He cast his mind briefly back to Dark Creek, to the cool interior of the barn, the coldness of the straw pile, the rocking bench on the porch and the cluck of laying hens.

Soon, he had reached the perimeter of the camp, approaching it from such an angle that the horses made a barrier between him and the fire. Peering round them he quickly counted nine men. There were the six he had already seen plus three more who lay, apparently asleep, in the shade of a wagon.

The horses were tied to three posts driven into the ground. Making sure no one was looking his way he sneaked up to the first post and untied the horses' reins. The animals ignored him and continued to eat the hay strewn on the ground at their feet. Again moving as quietly as he could, he crept forward and untied the remaining horses. Then he made his retreat.

About forty feet from the horses, Daniel paused. Keeping low, he picked up a stone about the size of a large walnut and threw it as hard as he could at the closest horse. The stone hit its rump, the animal instantly rising up on its hind legs in shock before breaking into a gallop. The other horses, jinxed by their companion, ran off in several directions.

'Hey!' Daniel heard the shout of one of Quantrill's Raiders above the noise of hooves. 'Th' 'orses! Quick, grab 'em an' tie 'em up!'

In a moment men were running everywhere, their hands grasping at the horses' reins as they ran past them. Shortly the animals were tethered to the posts again.

'What's spooked 'em?' one of the men cried out.

This was Daniel's cue and, in response, he stood up and ran down the canyon as fast as his legs would take him.

'There, that kid!' a voice screamed over Daniel's shoulder. 'Come on, get 'im!'

Daniel ran from side to side, hoping he would not

be an easy target. He could hear Quantrill's Raiders shouting and cursing as they pursued him. Suddenly, a rock on the canyon wall a few yards ahead of him exploded, followed by a sharp crack from behind. Summoning all his strength, he sprinted around the corner in the canyon and into the dead-end at the top of which, he hoped, No-Head, Beto and Jesus were lying in wait. His sides aching and his legs almost giving way beneath him, he made it to the far end and threw himself down behind an earth mound. He could hear Quantrill's Raiders following behind.

'He's in 'ere somewhere,' one of them said. 'There's no way out. Find 'im.'

Daniel held his breath. Why hadn't No-Head and the others opened fire? Had he run into the wrong dead-end? He could hear the outlaws advancing towards him.

Suddenly, a shot rang out from high above, followed moments later by others. Despite the dangers, Daniel could not help but raise his head to take a look. Lying motionless on the canyon floor were four of the Raiders. The others were crouching behind rocks or had thrown themselves against the canyon walls for shelter, their faces turned skywards searching for the origin of the gunfire.

Another volley rang out, the man closest to Daniel falling, the blood from his chest slowly staining his shirt red and flowing onto the bare earth. The remaining members of the gang were now firing more accurately towards the source of the bullets. The exchange of fire continued for several minutes, slugs screaming and whistling as they whizzed through the air. A prolonged gunfight, Daniel thought, had not been part of No-Head's plan, certainly not one with him stuck in the middle with no way to protect himself. And soon his friends would run out of ammunition.

Suddenly, Daniel felt the ground beneath him begin to tremble, the vibrations becoming stronger with every second that passed. Chancing a look down the dead-end, Daniel was just in time to see the first steer round the entrance to the canyon. It was running at full speed with its head down, waving its horns from side to side. Immediately behind it came another, then another, filling the width of the *arroyo* with pounding bovine muscle. Behind them, astride her horse, was Trinity, Daniel's Navy Colt in her hand, firing into the air, driving the herd forwards.

The four outlaws were ousted from their hiding places by the stampeding steers, the two men closest to the canyon entrance knocked to the floor and trampled, kicked and tossed about. Their comrades fled towards where Daniel was hiding. As the crack of rifles was heard from above one man fell, the other continuing to run, glancing back over his shoulder every pace or two in terror.

Making a split-second decision Daniel ran to the body of the man who had fallen close to him. He removed his pistol from its holster and, checking it was loaded, held it at arm's length, aiming it at the fleeing Raider and squeezing the trigger. Levelling the gun, Daniel fired a second time, hitting the man. The Raider stumbled. Kicking up a cloud of dust, he fell face first into the dirt, rolled and was still.

At the sound of gunshots ahead of them, the herd, confused and scared, slowed. Each animal began to stamp their hooves, snort and turn this way and that but ceased their charge.

Trinity rode up to Daniel, passing through the herd of agitated steers to reach him. Moments later No-Head, Beto and Jesus arrived.

'Are y' hurt, Daniel?' No-Head asked.

'No,' Daniel replied, his hands still shaking as the wave of adrenaline in his body subsided.

No-Head turned to Trinity. 'That was a dangerous thing t' do,' he chastized her. 'Th' steers could've been hurt, not to mention you.'

'I knew that,' she replied, 'but all I was hearing was gunfire so I figured that y' needed an advantage, something t' break th' deadlock in your favour. This was all I could think of.' Trinity hung her head and looked at her hands holding the reins in her lap.

'Y're a brave girl, Trinity, an' that shows some clever thinking,' No-Head continued, 'but don't y' do that again. Your ma an' pa'd never let me back on t' Dark Creek if theys knew what I let y' do.'

Trinity looked up. 'No, sir, I promise.'

'Good girl,' No-Head said. 'Now, give Daniel

back his gun an' let's check out these vermin an' their camp.'

Trinity did as she was told. As she turned her horse, Daniel caught a glimpse of No-Head smiling and winking at her. She smiled back. Although he could not say as much, Daniel knew No-Head was proud of her quick thinking.

While Trinity, Beto and Jesus looked after the herd, No-Head and Daniel checked the bodies of the outlaws. No-Head searched each man methodically, turning up a few dollars, two knives and a pair of boots that he fancied for himself. They seized the rifles and guns as well, hoping to be able to sell them once they reached Kansas City.

No-Head took Daniel back to where Satan was still tethered and together they cautiously rode to the Raiders' camp. It was deserted, the fire smouldering. Searching the wagon, they found a few cans of food, some blankets and a small amount of ammunition, all of which they decided to take with them. At the back of the wagon, Daniel discovered a small wooden chest with a lock on the front.

'Bring it down here,' No-Head ordered. Daniel placed it on the ground.

Taking his gun from its holster, No-Head shot the lock from the chest, its lid springing open. Inside was a small pistol, eight rounds of ammunition and a quantity of banknotes. Counting it, Daniel found it to be just over four hundred dollars.

'That'll be the money stolen from them homesteaders,' No-Head said pensively. 'Take it, Daniel.'

'But it's not my money,' Daniel said. Simply by holding it he felt sullied, like he had been the one who had killed Ted Scupham for it.

'An' it ain't no one else's now either,' No-Head replied enigmatically. 'I ain't never seen a buzzard or a ghila monster drinking moonshine or dealing the pastes.'

Daniel took the money and guiltily stuffed it into his saddlebag.

After three quarters of an hour, Beto and Trinity arrived, driving the steers through the canyons to the other side of the hills. Behind them came Jesus and the wagon, Roja asleep in the back. They loaded what supplies they had discovered in the

Raiders' camp and tied two unbranded horses to the back of the wagon to take with them. By nightfall, they had passed safely through the hills and were once more engulfed by the tranquillity of the prairie lands, the terror of the day already feeling a world away.

Chapter 11

★

JOURNEY'S END

For several days they rode on, meeting nobody and seeing few signs of life other than Indian habitation: campsites around hearths filled with old charcoal, the ground scattered with half-made stone arrow-heads. At one point Daniel, riding at the head of the herd, crested a hill to be confronted by an amazing vista. At least ten thousand buffalo were sauntering slowly through the grass beneath him. They reminded him of boats riding at anchor in the Thames estuary off Chatham, all pointing in the same direction as if being positioned by tidal currents and wind. As the steers mingled with the bison, the wild animals separated to give way to them. Roja, recovering well from his mauling by the mountain lion, rode on the wagon seat, sitting up next to Jesus, who joked that it was as if the dog were riding shotgun.

On the fifth day, Daniel saw in the distance what appeared to be buildings. Drawing closer he realized they were farmsteads, but they looked nothing like the Gravitts' home. These were built of stone and painted wood with neat white picket fences hemming in manicured grass lawns. Soon he could discern a town ahead. It was Kansas City, journey's end.

Camping some miles outside the town limits, No-Head spoke to Daniel at first light. 'Let's head on in. Much as I don't like it, we got t' go t' Camp Union if we want to sell these beeves. Jus' remember, this is a Blue Belly town so keep alert.'

The two of them rode off into town, leaving the others with the herd.

After so many weeks on the trail, it seemed

strange to Daniel to see so many buildings again. There was a large Catholic church, a brickyard, shops, houses, a mayor's office and even an office publishing the town's newspaper, the *Kansas City Times*. The Missouri River was lined with warehouses, hotels and saloons. He was surprised to see that there were a large number of Indians living in the town. Furthermore, they appeared to be rather wealthy: most of them had given up wearing buckskins and were dressed in white men's clothing, even so far as to sport waistcoats, well-tailored pants, top hats and boots. One or two displayed a gold watch-chain on their chests.

Daniel and No-Head approached Camp Union in the centre of town. With its tall rectangular walls and guardhouse made from stone and wood it had a commanding view of the river.

Dismounting and leading their horses forwards they walked towards a sentry by the camp's main gate. The guard studied them for a moment and lowered his rifle from his shoulder.

'Hold still and state your business,' he commanded.

'We're lookin' for th' officer in charge of purchasing supplies,' No-Head replied, looking him straight in the eye.

The sentry seemed simultaneously confused and alarmed. He had clearly noticed No-Head's Texan drawl.

'We don't deal with Rebs,' the sentry said dismissively, pointing the bayonet of his rifle at No-Head's chest.

'We're not Rebels,' Daniel said. 'We just want to sell our beeves.'

The guard looked even more confused. Daniel's accent was even stranger to him.

'Stand aside!' The sentry signalled to a comrade within the fort.

'You got a problem, Jeremiah?'

'I got two problems. Two Rebs that speak right funny.'

The second guard approached, cocking his weapon as he came. Together, the two Blue Bellies searched Daniel and No-Head's saddlebags.

'You can pass,' the first sentry finally said. He motioned to a building behind him inside the camp's perimeter. 'Tether your horses and hand your weapons in to the guardhouse. Someone'll deal with you.'

No-Head and Daniel walked past the sentries and into the camp. Inside, Daniel saw that the place was much larger than he had expected. Arranged in a row were seven large bullock wagons being loaded with supplies. Sacks of flour, boxes of ammunition and stacks of rifles lay piled in heaps. There was a sizeable corral in one corner of the yard, enclosed by a post-and-rail fence. Four steers and three horses stood in it. Beside the corral was a blockhouse with smoke rising from a metal chimney. From the odours drifting through the building's open door, Daniel assumed this was the camp's cookhouse: the aroma of steak and kidney pie made his mouth water. To one side of the door a young soldier with his sleeves rolled up was peeling potatoes with a clasp knife. Arranged around the compound were other buildings. Through a window in one Daniel could see rows of bunk beds. On a small platform near the centre of the fort stood a cannon, its muzzle pointing north-east. There were soldiers everywhere engaged in military chores. Few of them paid Daniel and No-Head any attention.

'Looks to me,' No-Head said in a quiet voice, 'like we's got us a real Blue Bellies hornets' nest here.'

Once they had tied up their horses and relinquished their weapons, they were shown into the quartermaster's office. He was a tall, thin, elderly man, his skin as tanned as leather from years of active service. His brown eyes were weak and almost colourless and his teeth yellowed from years of chewing tobacco. As they walked in he spat a large gob of brown saliva into a brass spittoon by the end of his desk.

'I'm Lieutenant Gregory. I seed you comin'. Y' got beeves t' sell?' the officer asked curtly.

'Yes, sir,' No-Head answered. 'We got us fifty head. We also got two horses if y're int'rested.'

'Not interested in th' horses, might be in th' beeves,' he responded. 'Where y' from?'

'South aways,' No-Head replied.

Lieutenant Gregory looked at No-Head, then to Daniel. 'Got a name of th' place?'

'Mound City,' Daniel replied. 'It's north of the Red River.'

'Never heard of it,' said the quartermaster. 'Don't reckon I'm likely t' have either. Some flea-bit place b'tween the Devil an' th' deep blue.' He reached across his desk and picked up a piece of paper on which was written a tariff list. 'Y' fatten them up some, start t' get a bit of meat back on 'em an' in a week I'll give y' thirty bucks a head f' your beeves. That's, of course, assuming they pass muster when I sees 'em.'

Thirty dollars! Daniel had to stop himself blurting it out in amazement.

'That'll do fine, sir,' No-Head said without betraying a trace of emotion. 'One week from t'day we'll return t' Camp Union an' complete th' business.'

The quartermaster spat again, another gob of spittle chiming on the brass rim of the spittoon and sliding down to join the noxious contents. 'Close th' door as y' go.'

As they rode out of the fort and through the town,

No-Head suddenly asked, 'Y' know what's good after weeks on th' trail, Daniel?'

Daniel thought for a moment and said, 'Sleeping in a bed?'

'No,' said No-Head. 'Better than that. Y' come with me.'

They stopped and tied their horses up outside a building with a notice across the front reading *Ah Chong – Chinese Laundry and Bathhouse*. Pushing through the swing door after No-Head, Daniel found himself confronted by a Chinese man, his hair in a long pigtail and wearing a black silk skull-cap with a red button on the top. He was seated behind a desk upon which lay a pile of large white towels.

'Yoo wanchee bafoo, master?' he asked.

'Wanchee bafoo an' laundry,' replied No-Head.

'Two piece?' the Chinese asked, pointing from No-Head to Daniel.

'Two piece,' No-Head confirmed.

Another Chinese man appeared to lead them down a corridor and into a large room in the centre of which stood two enamel hip baths.

238

'Number one service? Number two service?' the Chinese man asked.

Without asking Daniel his opinion, No-Head answered, 'Number one service two time.'

The Chinese man disappeared to return with buckets of steaming water, which he poured into the baths, putting bars of jasmine-scented soap on the floor by each. No-Head stripped his clothes off and lowered himself into the bath with a heartfelt sigh. Daniel did likewise. The hot water was sheer luxury. He could not remember when he had last had a bath. Yet another Chinese man entered the room and picked up their clothes, emptying their pockets and putting their contents on a side table with their guns. Daniel slid down under the water, closing his eyes. He could almost feel the dust and grime of the trail leaching from his pores, his every aching muscle loosening and stretching as if in a peaceful sleep. When he broke the surface again, he met with a surprise. Standing next to the hip bath was a woman, her long hair piled up in billows on her head like cumulus clouds, held in place by mother-of-pearl combs. She was wearing a basque decorated with little red ribbons. Without a word, she picked up the bar of soap and began to lather Daniel's body all over. Across the room, another woman was doing likewise to No-Head.

'Now, this is what I call luxury!' No-Head remarked. He reached out for the side table where a fat cigar lay in a brass ashtray. He puffed at it, a cloud of smoke rising to mix with the steam.

Half an hour later, the Chinese laundryman returned with Daniel's clothes. Daniel swung his leg over the edge of the bath and tugged his clothing on, his shirt sticking to his back.

No-Head, still lying back in the water, looked across to Daniel and said, 'Y' see my leather poke over there? Y' take two silver dollars out 'f that, go down aways t' th' saloon an' get yerself a good meal. I'll settle up with th' Chinee an' I'll join y' shortly.'

As Daniel left the room, he saw No-Head kiss on the cheek the girl who had been washing him.

The saloon was crowded but Daniel found a small table, sat down and, when the aproned waiter approached him, ordered a plate of fried chicken and squash. It was a welcome break from Jesus's trail food. To accompany it, he ordered a glass of beer. As he ate, he studied the clientele of the saloon. At one table there were half a dozen Blue Bellies. Watching them, he realized that they were his enemy. It seemed strange: they looked just like any other men, save for their uniforms. Also present were some jayhawkers, speaking loudly about the evils of slavery. At the far end of the saloon were three or four Negroes who, Daniel realized, must be recently freed slaves. They looked uneasy.

After No-Head had joined him and they had finished their meals, they left the saloon together and walked along the boardwalk. Ahead of them was gathered a group of men around a table hung with a velvet cloth edged with gold braid. On the table stood a box covered as might be a magician's hat with a rectangle of black cotton. Leaning over it was a tall, austere-looking man wearing a top hat and a tail coat.

'Step up, step up!' he called out. 'Come and see one of the marvels of the natural world. It has bemused the crowned heads of Europe. It has left

Queen Victoria of England breathless in wonder. The Emperor of France himself has offered a thousand gold pieces for it. I am Doctor Belldecker, proprietor, trainer and organizer of Belldecker's Internationally Famous Flea Circus. Never before have such wonders been seen in the Americas.' In front of the box he placed a very large magnifying glass on a stand. 'Before I display this wonder of the animal kingdom, may I please ask for a contribution towards the upkeep of this marvel. Might I suggest a suitable sum to be deposited in the hat before you is but a dime. This will be the best one bit's entertainment you will ever purchase in your lives.'

Outstretched hands deposited coins in the hat. Daniel, filled with curiosity, added his.

'Are we all done?' asked Doctor Belldecker. 'Very well.' He put his hand on the cloth covering the box. 'Prepare to be amazed.'

With a flourish he displayed a glass box about the size of a family Bible standing on its end. Within, stretched across the middle, was a thin wire, the interior of the glass box being painted to resemble a circus ring. Ranged along the wire were a number of tiny figures, each about the size of a grain of rice, painted as if wearing clothes. Elsewhere in the box, Daniel could see a lot of small dots jumping haphazardly about.

'Observe,' said the circus owner.

He vibrated the wire through the end of the box with his thumbnail. As the wire twanged, the little figures flew into the air, alarming the real fleas, which rose from the floor of the cage in a reddish-brown cloud. Just looking at them made Daniel itch. Doctor Belldecker made a little bow and dropped the cloth over the box.

'And now, ladies and gentlemen, before we depart with reminiscences of this remarkable exposition, may I introduce you to something as wonderful.'

He took a brown six-sided bottle out of his coat pocket, its mouth sealed with a cork held in place by red sealing wax.

'This,' he said, 'is Doctor Ching's Elixir, straight from the Chinese laboratories of San Francisco. A tincture of the poppy, it is an assured cure for an upset stomach, toothache, the ravages of influenza, sleeplessness, gout and many other common ailments. It will help Baby to sleep, it will soothe a fractious child. It is in short the modern medicine we have all been waiting for. Today only, for this present august company, it is but one dollar a bottle.'

Daniel, although somewhat sceptical, bought a bottle. Tad would be teething by the time they returned to Dark Creek and the liquid might come in handy.

'Y' been suckered?' No-Head asked.

'No,' Daniel replied defensively. 'He said the medicine is good for babies.'

'An' a bullet's good for a rabid dog,' replied No-Head, 'but I bet its mother wouldn't buy a gun.'

Throughout the next seven days, they grazed the herd on a pasture about six miles south-east of Kansas City, beyond the extent of the plots that the townsfolk tended for growing food and beyond the last of the farms. While the cattle ate their fill there was some time to relax, though Jesus and Beto stayed with the herd. They feared the welcome a couple of Mexicanos might get this far from the southern border territories. No-Head visited the livery stable and sold the horses and guns they had taken from Quantrill's Raiders. Thereafter, he spent most of his free time in the saloon where, Daniel was sure, he was attempting to make this an even more profitable trip. Trinity took to wandering along the main streets, gazing wide-eyed at the quantity and diversity of the goods displayed in the numerous shops, especially the draper's.

''portant lesson,' No-Head had said. 'If there's a shop that sells baubles an' bangles an' beads, y' can be sure th' ladies 's flyin' around it like ants t' a nest on a rainy day.'

Once Daniel had seen the town he started exploring the surrounding area. About four miles south of the main settlement was Campbell Town, a rather grand name for what amounted to a handful of houses. These were clustered around a central single-storey building roughly made of stone and logs. Daniel tied his horse to a rail beneath a sign on the building that read MISSION OF THE SOCIETY OF FRIENDS, and headed inside.

The interior of the building was divided into a number of rooms accessed off a central passageway. Daniel noticed the rooms were furnished sparsely, the furniture carved out of wood and lacking any form of ornamentation at all. Indeed, the only decorations to be found anywhere were small paintings depicting religious scenes and numerous wooden and metal icons. At one end was a chapel full of wooden pews.

Going down the corridor Daniel knocked on the door of what seemed to be an office. A voice bade him enter. Inside was a man in a shabby black suit seated at a desk making entries with a scratchy nib into a leather-bound ledger. On the desk was a small wooden box and an inkpot.

'Hello, son. May I help you, friend?' the man asked in a soft, welcoming voice.

'I'm looking for the . . .' Daniel wondered what the head of a mission would be called. 'Pastor.'

The man smiled. 'You found him. My name is Tom Greenleaf.'

'I am Daniel Chance,' Daniel replied, holding his hand out. The pastor took it and they shook hands.

The skin on his fingers was rough from manual labour.

'Now, what is it that I can do for you, my son?'

'I wish to make a donation,' Daniel replied, removing the roll of notes he had taken from Quantrill's Raiders from his pocket and handing it to the pastor.

'That is a mighty load of money, young Daniel.' Mr Greenleaf turned the roll of banknotes over in his hand. 'More than our mission possesses. We are Quakers and live simple lives according to the word of Our Lord.'

'I know,' replied Daniel. 'But the money belonged to a Quaker gentleman, a Mr Scupham. He was robbed of it and I and my friends robbed the robbers. I think it would have been his wish for the money to be paid to his church.'

Mr Greenleaf looked up at Daniel. 'You are a true Christian, my boy. There are not many who would turn their back on such a temptation.'

Opening the wooden box that lay upon his desk, the pastor placed the money inside and closed the lid once again, the lock clicking solidly.

As Daniel passed a classroom with two rows of children seated before a blackboard, a teacher wearing an ankle-length black robe began to conduct them. In high voices they sang to the tune of *Auld Lang Syne*:

> We cross the prairie as of old
> The Pilgrims crossed the sea,
> To make the west, as they the east,
> The homestead of the free.

After a week of grazing, the steers had started to put on weight and No-Head considered they could now be sold. He, Daniel and Trinity would take the herd into town while Beto and Jesus were to stay with the camp wagon at the place where the cattle had been pastured.

'Be sure,' No-Head ordered Beto and Jesus, 'y're ready t' move out the minute we get back.'

Despite the streets being wide and unpaved, the sight of fifty head of cattle walking through the centre of town seemed to unnerve the inhabitants. As the steers approached, lowing and defecating as they moved, pedestrians hurried to the safety of the raised boardwalk while mounted travellers, wagons and even a stagecoach moved to the side of the road to allow the herd to pass. At one point, No-Head detached himself from the procession and vanished down a side street, returning moments later with a small sack tied up with twine hanging from the horn of his saddle. Ominously, something in the sack was writhing and hissing. Daniel cast an inquisitive look at him.

'You'll learn soon enough,' No-Head replied mysteriously.

They reached the gates of Camp Union, the sentries opening them wide to allow the cattle to enter. Slowly the steers were guided across the compound and into the corral. Lieutenant Gregory walked out of the procurement office.

'Right, let's see these Red River beeves of yours.' He climbed into the corral and moved between the beasts. At each animal he paused, put his fingers in its nostrils, pulled its head back and studied its eyes, felt its flesh and ran his hand over its flanks, feeling for parasites. He climbed back over the fence.

'Not quite as plump as I had hoped.'

No-Head and Daniel exchanged a glance.

'But I'll take 'em,' Gregory continued. 'Y' care t' step into my office?'

No-Head dismounted and, handing the reins of his horse to Daniel, followed Gregory, disappearing into the building.

Daniel and Trinity sat on their horses in the middle of the camp. The sack on No-Head's horse still twitched spasmodically.

A few minutes later, No-Head stepped out of the quartermaster's office door. In his hand he held a small leather pouch which he put securely in his pocket. He winked at Daniel and Trinity.

'How much did we get?' Trinity asked.

'Thirty bucks a steer,' No-Head replied. His grin was wide.

He stepped across to his horse, put his left foot in the stirrup and swung himself into the saddle, taking the reins from Daniel.

'We ready?'

'We're ready,' Daniel agreed.

'Good,' No-Head said. He undid the drawstring

around the sack and reached into it. 'Get ready t' ride like y've just seen the ghost riders of th' Apocalypse!'

No-Head removed his hand. In it he held a black-and-white cat by the scruff of its neck. The cat jerked and wriggled, its claws slicing through the air. With a swing of his wrist, No-Head hurled the cat over his head and into the middle of the herd of cattle. With the agility of its species the cat landed on its feet, immediately running in frenzied circles through the forest of bovine legs. Within a few seconds the cattle were panicking, pressing against the fence of the corral in a frenzy. It gave way with a splintering crack. A moment later, they had burst out into the camp compound.

'Go!' No-Head urged Daniel and Trinity, and all three of them dug their spurs into their horses' sides. As they raced for the gate Daniel glanced over his shoulder.

The camp was in chaos. Soldiers had discarded their duties. Even the main gate sentries had abandoned their posts. Sacks lay where they had been trampled or tossed, the air dense with a fog of flour. Piles of boxes had been pushed over and smashed; provisions and ammunition were scattered everywhere. Stacks of rifles had been toppled, the barrels bent out of shape and their stocks splintered. Everywhere, men dived for cover from the hooves and horns. Out of the corner of his eye, Daniel saw one steer enter through an open doorway into the barracks.

Daniel, Trinity and No-Head rode on at speed, reaching the edge of town in a matter of minutes. Before long, they reached the rendezvous with Beto and Jesus, Kansas City disappearing in the dust behind them.

After an hour, No-Head felt that they had put enough distance between themselves and Camp Union, allowing them to ease up their pace. Sensing that they were out of danger, at least for now, the mood lightened and No-Head's face broke into a broad smirk.

'Thirty bucks a head! Not a bad price considerin'. An' by the time they round that lot up they'll have lost a bit more flesh. Good day's business all round, I'd say.'

* * *

The journey back from Kansas was long and hard. They kept alert and cautious throughout, conscious of the fact No-Head was carrying the entire profits of their enterprise, over one and half thousand dollars. Each day they covered as many miles as possible, keeping off well-used track ways and avoiding their former campsites.

After six weeks of riding and Dark Creek only a day away, they came across a military convoy of wagons and horses. Confederate Army troops, forlorn and tired, their faces soured with defeat, traipsed along the trail in procession. In the backs of the wagons, either sitting on the floor or lying on paliasses, were wounded soldiers, bloody bandages wrapped around them. Several of them had stumps where limbs had been amputated.

No-Head approached one of the outriders.

'Where y'all headin'?'

'Laredo,' the soldier replied. 'We're takin' these men back t' their homes. They ain't goin' t' be fightin' in this war again.'

As they passed each wagon Trinity looked at the

injured. At the fourth wagon she slowed her horse. Her face contorting with anguish, she asked quietly, 'Papa?'

In the back of the wagon was Matt. His face was soiled and his clothes torn, except for the patches Molly had sewn onto them, and he clutched the satchel that Beto had made for him. His Colt was at his side but his rifle was gone. A dirty bandage covered him from his ribs to his waist.

Matt called forward and the wagon pulled up. As Trinity dismounted, he climbed down with difficulty. 'My little girl!' he exclaimed as their arms entwined.

'Papa, you're hurt,' Trinity sobbed, afraid that her hug might cause him pain.

Matt smiled. 'It looks worse than it is. Come on, let's go home.'

Waving the convoy goodbye, Matt was helped up to sit by Jesus. As they moved off, he described what had happened to him. 'After my last seein' you, I went back to Austin and was posted to Arkansas. Given command o' my own unit. My orders was to take my men north into Missouri mixin' with ten thousand other Confederates under the command of General Benjamin McCulloch at Wilson's Creek, near Springfield. It was a whole lot of men, bigger than any herd of cattle I'd ever seen.' He chuckled and tried to scratch under his bandage as they headed down a smaller trail, away from the convoy.

'As dawn broke on the second day, them Blue Bellies attacked both north and south. We lost a lot o' men. I was ordered t' counterattack under cover of artillery fire. Them Blue Bellies didn't know what crushed 'em. After, I didn't wait for my orders, I took my men north. Two attacks on the Blue Bellies had already failed and we charged forth as part o' th' third offensive.' He looked at Trinity and explained, 'It was there I took a slug in th' side. But I been lucky. It just went straight on through.' He winked, indicating that she should not worry.

'Heard the Blue Bellies were forced to retreat. The Confederates holdin' their ground.' Matt sighed, shaking his head. 'I think we might have won th' battle but heard we lost two hundred men with another nine hundred wounded. Can't help but feel it weren't a real victory.'

'At least you're goin' to be all right, Papa,' Trinity said.

Matt nodded in agreement. 'Now, y' know, on th' journey home, I heard tell of some happenin's in Kansas City. It seems some beeves stampeded in Camp Union. They smashed up mos' o' th' supplies and equipment they had, caused a load o' mess. Got int' the cookhouse and barracks too: th' Blue Bellies were picking cow patties out o' their bunks for days!' He smiled knowingly. 'Y' wouldn't happen t' know anything about that, would y'?'

The following morning, three hours after they broke camp, the gates of Dark Creek ranch welcomed them home. Roja, his tail flicking, leaped down from No-Head's horse and sped towards the farm, barking an excited greeting. As they passed through the gates, Molly yanked open the house door, running to meet them. Moments later May-Anne and a bawling Tad appeared. Even El Sueño was full of energy and happy to see them.

As the others jumped from their saddles, glad to be back, Daniel stroked Satan's neck, smoothing a ruffled patch of the horse's coat. Leaning forwards he whispered, 'We made it, Satan. We're back home.'

Home. The word somehow sounded strange. Ever since he had left England he had travelled but never revisited anywhere, never returned to anyone. Yet as Molly called for him to dismount, her arms tightly hugging Matt and Trinity, Daniel knew that, until he found his parents, they would be his family and Dark Creek his home.

Glossary

Note: Mexican is more correctly a form of Spanish but is here referred to as the former.

aces over threes a high hand in the card game of poker: called a 'full house', it consists of two cards of one suit and three of another; in No-Head Nolan's case [page 16], three aces and two threes

adobe [pron. *add-oh-bee*] a method of building using wood and mud made from fine or sieved soil

Anglos white men who were not of Mexican origin

Apache an Indian tribe, one of the largest

Arkansas [pron. *Are-can-saw*]

arroyo dried bed of a small stream

bandanna a small scarf, often red in colour, worn by cowboys around the throat

bandito [pron. *ban-dee-toe*] a Mexican bandit

bar-keep a barman

beeves cattle, the Texas plural of beef

Beto [pron. *Bet-oh*] short for Alberto (Albert)

binder a low-class person, usually crooked; also a hired killer

bloody flux dysentery

Blue Bellies Union (northern states) troops who wore dark blue uniform jackets

blue norther a bitingly cold wind that blows down over Texas from the snow-covered middle of America in the winter months

Bob-white a Bob-white quail, a game bird then common in south Texas

bourbon American whiskey

brasada see *brush popper*

brave an Indian warrior

brush popper a cowboy who worked in the Texan brush country (the *brasada*)

buck a dollar

buckaroo a mean, trail-toughened cowboy

buenas noches [pron. *bwone-as notch-ess*] goodnight

bull chips cow pats; cattle dung. When dry, it was sometimes used as fuel

bumper-brim a close-fitting hat that vaguely resembles an upturned pudding bowl; it has a very small brim

bunkhouse a sort of dormitory for *vaqueros* and ranch hands, a separate building from the ranch house

bunko a card (sometimes dice) game, often crooked and run by card sharps (*qv*)

bunko steerer a decoy in a bunko game, employed to distract the players from seeing they are being cheated

burro [pron. *boo-row*] a mule

Caddoes and **Wacoes** Indians of the small Caddo and Waco tribes in Texas

card sharp a cheat at cards, often a professional swindler

castrated castration is the act of removing a male animal's testicles; it is done to calm the animal

down as well as to stop it
breeding. In cattle, it also
helps to fatten them up

Chaparral an area of land of
very dense scrub oak,
mesquite, cacti and vine
cover

chips see *bull chips*

Comanche an Indian tribe,
one of the largest

compadre comrade

Confederates troops of the
Confederate (southern
states) army

corral a fenced livestock
enclosure

cottonmouth a water
moccasin, one of North
America's most deadly
snakes; so-called after its
white mouth

cottontail a rabbit

cow-poke (or **-puncher**) a
derogatory term for a
cowboy or *vaquero*

coyote [pron. *coy-oat-ee* but,

in Texas, sometimes
k-eye-oat] a wild dog like
a large jackal; sometimes
referred to as a prairie
wolf

crackers dry biscuits like
modern plain cheese
biscuits

crutches-and-bar two iron
posts shaped like a Y with
a crossbar, used for sus-
pending pots or meat over
a cooking fire

curandero the Mexican
Indian equivalent of a
witchdoctor

Derby [pron. *dur-bee*] a
bowler hat with a narrow
rim

dogie [pron. *doh-gee* (*gee* as
in *geek*)] a calf, often an
orphaned calf

dubbin a paste made of
beeswax and various oils,
it preserves and polishes

leather and keeps it supple
duck a coarse material rather
   like canvas or heavy
   denim

El Sueño The Sleeper
ewer a pitcher or large jug

Fredo [pron. *Frey-doh*] short
   for Alfredo (Alfred)

galleta [pron. *gay yey-tah*] a
   nutritious grass
'gator alligator
grizzly a bear

hardtack a hard biscuit like a
   ship's biscuit; it had to be
   soaked in liquid before it
   could be eaten
huajillo [pron. *wah-hee-yo*]
   a large bush that grows in
   south Texas; much
   favoured as food by cattle

jack rabbit a hare

javelina the North American
   wild boar, more properly
   known as a collared
   peccary
jayhawker a Kansas guerrilla
   during the Civil War who
   supported the Union
jerky strips of raw beef
   preserved by wind-drying
   in the sun
Jesus [pron. *Hey-soos*] a
   common male given name
   in Roman Catholic
   Mexico
Johnny Reb a slang name
   for a Confederate soldier
   (*abbr.* of Johnnie Rebel)

(a) left and a right shooting
   two animals, one with
   each barrel of a double-
   barrelled shotgun in quick
   succession
long-johns the usual cowboy
   underwear; it consisted of
   a one-piece, vest-cum-

underpants-like garment made of cotton or wool. It was buttoned up the front from the groin to the neck with long sleeves and legs reaching to the elbows and knees.

lucifer a match; it could be struck against any rough surface, not just the side of the box like modern safety matches

mariachi [pron. *marry-are-chee*] a form of Mexican folk music played mainly on guitars

marlinspike a metal spike used to undo very tight knots in ropes

mesquite [pron. *muss-keet*] a low, often contorted tree with very hard wood; the seeds can be ground into a nutritious meal

Mexxie a derogatory word for a Mexican

Miguel [pron. *Mee-gwell*] Mexican/Spanish for Michael

moccasin an Indian form of footwear; also slang for a water moccasin, also known as a cottonmouth (*qv*)

mustang a wild, untamed horse

negra a Negro; black people were called Negroes, from the Spanish word for 'black'. It was not considered a racial slur, but the slang word 'nigger', derived from it, was later to become so

offal the parts of an animal that are often not eaten such as intestines

ostler a man who tends horses in a livery stable

263

pan lake

pants rats parasitic human body lice; also known as *seam squirrels*

pastes playing cards

pemmican an American Indian food, especially made from bison meat by the tribes of the Great Plains; Anglos also made it for themselves with bison meat or beef

pilot bread a hard type of bread-cum-biscuit similar to hardtack

pistoliero a gunman

poncho a short, all-purpose and often weatherproof woollen cape with a hole in it for the neck, worn by Mexican men (not to be confused with a *serape*)

Quantrill's Raiders a ruthless, sometimes pro-Confederate, band of men who, after the war, mostly became outlaws

rattler a rattlesnake

reach a piece of wood holding a wagon's axles together

riata [pron. *ree-art-ah*] otherwise commonly known as a *lasso*, a stiff looped rope thrown to catch cattle or horses

Rio Grande the river that divides Texas from Mexico

road runner a large bird of the cuckoo family that runs rather than flies; it eats snakes

roja red

runt the weakest animal in a litter

San Antone the slang name for the south Texas town of San Antonio

264

sarsaparilla [pron. *sar-suh-puh-rilla*] a popular, often fizzy, non-alcoholic drink made from the roots of the smilax vines. Also known as root beer

señor [pron. *sain-yor*] a word of respect similar to *sir*

señorito [pron. *sain-yor-eet-oh*] a slang word, it was roughly equivalent to *little sir* – it is no longer in common usage

serape a blanket worn by both Mexican men and women as a kind of shawl

sharp see **card sharp**

siesta a rest, usually taken in the middle of the day when the sun is at its height

skeeters mosquitoes

sod a tuft of living grass in a lump of soil used as roofing

sombrero [pron. *som-brare-oh*] a wide-brimmed hat with upturned edges commonly worn by Mexican men

Stars 'n' Bars the American flag; it was the flag of the Union states in the American Civil War

Tejano a Texan (Spanish)

tenderpaw someone used to an easy life; also a **tenderfoot**, meaning someone who is inexperienced

tepee a conical Indian tent

twister tornado

vaquero [pron. *vak-air-oh*] the Mexican/south Texan word for a cowboy

white-tail a common deer which snorts through its nostrils when alarmed